As I was climbing up the stair
I met a man who wasn't there.
He wasn't there again today.
Oh, how I wish he'd go away.

TRIPPER & SAM

The Ghost Who Wanted To Be a Star

TRIPPER & SAM

The Ghost Who Wanted To Be a Star

Nancy K. Robinson

AN
APPLE
PAPERBACK

SCHOLASTIC INC.
New York Toronto London Auckland Sydney

ISBN 0-590-33595-2

Copyright © 1987 by Nancy K. Robinson. All rights reserved. Published by Scholastic Inc. APPLE PAPERBACKS is a registered trademark of Scholastic Inc.

12 11 10 9 8 7 6 5 4 3 2 1   7 8 9/8 0 1 2/9

Printed in the U.S.A.   01

First Scholastic printing, April 1987

To Toria Rance,
my favorite pixy. . . .

Special Acknowledgment

This book could not have been written without the expertise of Gene De Fever, David Eisendrath, and Richard Waddell.

PROLOGUE

Sam was Tripper's oldest friend. She had known him since she was a little girl. They had met one summer afternoon in Central Park.

It was a story they had both heard many times. . . .

Tripper's father, a documentary film director, had been shooting a film at the model boat lake. Every day a boy showed up on his bicycle to watch the filming.

One afternoon Tripper arrived with her grandmother. She was clutching a small boat made of popsicle sticks.

"Whatever you do," her grandmother warned her, "don't fall in the lake."

Tripper took one look at her grandmother, ran to the deep end of the lake, and fell in.

Before anyone realized what had happened, the boy dropped his bicycle and ran to the spot where Tripper had disappeared. He lay down at the edge, reached in, and pulled Tripper out. He almost fell in himself.

Tripper lay on the ground, soaking wet. Her eyes were closed. She wasn't moving. The boy began pressing his hand on her stomach . . .

". . . the way I've seen them do on those rescue shows on TV," he explained to a newspaper reporter later on. Water came out of Tripper's mouth.

"Are you breathing?" the boy asked her.

"No!" Tripper screamed and she began to cry.

The young hero was named Sam. Sam did not want a reward for saving Tripper's life. He just wanted to be allowed to hang around the film office after school. He wanted to learn how movies were made. . . .

The Rules of Conduct

"Listen to this, Tripper. There are Rules of Conduct for Meeting a Ghost." Katy Bear had her head buried in a book called *The Dictionary of the Supernatural*. She hadn't once looked out the window of the taxi as they drove in from the airport, even though it was her first visit to New York City.

Katy Bear was Tripper's best friend from boarding school in Colorado. For some reason she was always called by her first and last name. Tripper, on the other hand, was only called by her last name. Katy Bear was visiting her aunt in New York City for the first week of summer vacation.

" 'Rule number one,' " Katy Bear went on, " 'Do not move, and *on no account* ap-

3

proach the figure. Rule number two: If the figure speaks, do not approach, but try to find out its name, age, origin, and cause of visit if in trouble. . . .' " She looked over at Tripper.

"Tripper," she said, "are you listening?"

Tripper was gazing out at the skyline as they came across the 59th Street Bridge. She shook her head. "I'm not going to meet a ghost."

"Of course you are," Katy Bear said. "You're going to Scotland."

"There's more in Scotland than ghosts." Tripper noticed a line of dark clouds that seemed to be moving fast across the East River. It felt good to be home, even though it was only for a few hours. She was leaving later that night to join her father and his film crew on an island off the west coast of Scotland.

"Besides," Tripper went on, "Dad's not making a film about ghosts; he's making a film about diving for treasure on sunken wrecks all over the world. He's on the Isle of Mull, filming the biggest salvage operation ever done on the Tobermory Galleon."

"What's the Tobermory Galleon?" Katy Bear asked.

"It's a ship that was part of the Spanish Armada," Tripper told her. "It blew up and sank in Tobermory Bay in 1588."

"Four hundred years ago?" Katy Bear's eyes opened wide. "Well, then, of course there will be ghosts hanging around. Spanish ghosts most likely. You'd better take a Spanish dictionary. And there's probably a curse, too."

"A what?" Tripper asked.

"A curse," Katy Bear said, "like the Curse of the Mummy's Tomb. It always happens when you start digging up the past, messing around with history. Things start to happen."

"What sort of things?" Tripper was amused.

"Terrible things," Katy Bear said cheerfully, and went on reading. " 'Do not move until figure disappears. Note exact method of vanishing. If through an open doorway, quietly follow. If through a solid object, such as a wall. . . .' "

Suddenly the sky lit up with lightning, and there was a loud crash of thunder. The taxi turned off the 59th Street Bridge.

Katy Bear looked up. "Oh," she said. "I guess we're almost there," and she closed the book. She turned to Tripper. "Do you think I'm finally going to meet Sam?" Then she noticed that Tripper was staring at her.

"Katy Bear, you just stopped right in the middle of a sentence."

"Go on. Go on," the taxi driver called over his shoulder. "Do you follow him through a wall or not?"

"Who?" Katy Bear asked.

"The ghost," the taxi driver said impatiently.

Katy Bear opened the book, found the page again, and skimmed it quickly. "No," she said. "You just check to see if it's visible on the other side."

The taxi driver nodded.

By the time they pulled up in front of Tripper's townhouse, the rain was coming down in sheets. Tripper paid the taxi driver and he helped them out with their bags.

The townhouse was on the corner of East 50th Street and Beekman Place on a bluff overlooking the East River. The lower floors were used as Roger Tripper's film offices. Tripper and her father shared an apartment on the top floor.

Tripper and Katy Bear dumped their

bags in the front hall. The ground floor was dark except for a flickering light coming from the cutting room at the end of the hall.

"Is that you, Tripper?" a voice called.

"Hi, Eva!"

Tripper led Katy Bear down the dark hallway to the editing room. Katy Bear stared at the shelves of film cans that lined the wall. She'd never been in a film office before.

Eva was sitting at the editing machine. Tripper gave her a big hug and turned to Katy Bear. "This is Eva, my father's film editor."

"I know." Katy Bear smiled at Eva. "I know all about Eva."

Over the years, Katy Bear had heard about all the members of Roger Tripper's film crew — Coco, the electrician; Nick, the cameraman; Leroy, the unit manager. . . . In many ways the film crew had become Tripper's real family. Her mother had been a photojournalist who was killed on assignment when Tripper was only three years old.

"Is Sam here?" Katy Bear asked.

Eva smiled. "Sam will be back any minute. He went to get some of the wild sound Gene recorded in Scotland transferred to 35mm magnetic stripe film stock."

Ever since the day Sam had fished Tripper out of the lake in Central Park, he had worked in her father's film office after school. At first he just did errands and swept up, but Roger Tripper began to notice that Sam had an unusual talent for recording sound. He now worked as assistant sound man to Gene, the chief sound man, and went along on location during his vacations from high school.

Eva turned back to the editing machine. Her straight blonde hair swung back and forth as she worked.

"Come look at this shot," she said to Tripper. "It's the Western Isles Hotel. That's where you and Sam will be staying on the Isle of Mull."

Tripper and Katy Bear stood behind Eva so they could see the small screen.

It was a long shot of an old hotel on a cliff overlooking the harbor. As the camera tilted up, they saw a stone wall on a ledge that jutted out over the bay. Behind it was the Western Isles Hotel, which looked like a castle with its turrets and gables standing out against the evening sky. The wind was blowing the trees that surrounded the hotel.

"If this shot lasts long enough," Eva said, "I might be able to use it for the opening titles of this sequence. I'm going to look at it again."

As Eva rewound the film, Katy Bear whispered, "Tripper, did you happen to see a face in one of those windows?"

"No," Tripper said. "Did you?"

"No," Katy Bear said. "I just wondered if you did."

Eva started running the shot again.

The thunderstorm was still raging outside. The cutting room was dark and the rain beat hard against the windows. Katy Bear clutched Tripper's arm and stared at the screen. As the camera tilted up once again to the dark turrets of the Western Isles Hotel, Tripper felt a shiver go up her neck.

"Nice night for a murder," said a deep voice in her ear.

Spooks in the
Cutting Room

Tripper screamed and turned around.

"Very good," Sam said. "A scream *is* the next line. Now, if you can just name the movie, the studio, and the release date, you'll get twenty points."

Katy Bear was staring at Sam with her mouth open.

Tripper suddenly caught on. "Let me see," she said. "If the first line is 'Nice night for a murder,' and the next line is a scream . . . I know! *Scared Stiff* with Dean Martin and Jerry Lewis. Paramount Pictures. Release date: 1953."

She smiled at Sam. Sam was looking very well. He was wearing a yellow heavy-weather sailing jacket, blue jeans, and fisherman's boots. His reddish-gold curls were so wet, they looked dark.

Katy Bear nodded wisely. "I've heard about that game of yours."

It was a game Tripper and Sam had played for years. They called it Next Line. It always had to be a line from a famous motion picture.

"Not bad so far," Sam said.

"So far?" Tripper asked. "You mean there's more?"

All at once it came to her. "I know! It's a remake. It's a remake of *Ghostbreakers* with Bob Hope. Also Paramount. Release date: 1940. George Marshall directed both films."

"Excellent, Tripper." Sam was surprised. "You get another twenty points. Forty points in all."

"Well, we meet at last." Katy Bear had a habit of sounding like the gothic novels she was constantly reading. She asked Sam if he would like to come to her aunt's house for dinner. "Tripper's coming," she said. "We're taking her to the airport later tonight. We'll take you, too."

"Thanks," Sam said, "but I always spend the last night before a trip with Binker."

"Oh, I know all about Binker," Katy Bear said.

Tripper held her breath. She hoped Katy Bear wouldn't say too much. Tripper had never cared much for Binker. She could never understand what Sam saw in the dull black dog, who always seemed to be daydreaming or half asleep. She had often referred to Binker as "that lump" when speaking about him to Katy Bear.

But Katy Bear just said politely, "I'd certainly like to meet Binker in person sometime. Well, not 'in person' — you know what I mean."

Sam nodded and turned to Eva. "How is the footage from Scotland?"

Eva groaned. "It's a mess."

Tripper looked around the cutting room and noticed, for the first time, that camera reports were spread all over the tables. She was surprised. Eva was usually very well-organized; she had extremely neat habits. Eva's face was flushed. She looked happy and excited.

"Fritz is in town," Eva said. "I'm supposed to meet him in an hour."

"Fritz Katzenbach?" Katy Bear's eyes lit up. She knew Eva's boyfriend was a famous international soccer player. He traveled a lot and had fans all over the world.

Eva looked up at the clock. "But I'm afraid I'll never get out of here. I've been on the phone to Scotland and the lab here all day."

"What's wrong with the footage?" Sam asked.

"Everything," Eva said bluntly. "Some of it is fogged. There are flares, scratches...." She sighed. "There's a beautiful sequence of the fishing boats in Tobermory Bay at dawn, but it will all have to be reshot."

"Why?" Tripper asked.

"It's simply full of ghosts," Eva said matter-of-factly.

Katy Bear nodded. "I'm not the least bit surprised," she said.

"It's not what you're thinking," Tripper said quickly. "In photography 'ghosts' just means double images. It's usually a problem with the lens or the coating on the lens."

"Even so," Katy Bear said slowly, "have you considered the possibility that the film might be haunted?"

"No!" Eva laughed. "There's always an

explanation for these problems, and believe me, I've tracked every one of them down. Either it's a leak in the film holder or a leak in the black changing bag or else light was coming in through the viewfinder or there were problems at the lab or the film was X-rayed coming through Customs. . . ." Eva took a deep breath. "There's always a reason."

Eva turned back to the editing machine. "I just wish I could get one sequence under control. Sam, by any chance, did Gene record any wild sound of wind — howling wind? I thought I'd try it over this shot of the Western Isles Hotel. It might be very effective."

"*Wild* sound?" Katy Bear whispered. "What's that?"

"Sound that's recorded separately from picture," Tripper told her.

Sam went into the hall and returned with a roll marked WILD SOUND: HOWLING WIND. Eva was very pleased. Then he went to put the rest of the sound transfers away.

Eva strung up the roll of wild sound on the editing machine. She pushed a button. Almost at once some very strange noises came from the editing machine.

"What in the world is *that*?" Eva asked. She ran it back and played it again. It sounded like a voice, but the words didn't make any sense: "Uh snob snidsen pollisay sid syedtion. . . ."

Katy Bear got very excited. "I know!"

As it turned out, Katy Bear had just finished reading a book called *Voices from the Other World*.

"They often come over tapes," she explained, "and they always speak some foreign language. . . ."

"Nonsense," Eva said softly, but Katy Bear was too busy explaining to hear her. "It can be a message from a relative or even from another world. . . ."

"Sam!" Eva called. "Come here!"

She played the beginning of the tape for Sam.

"Oh yeah," Sam said. "Play it backward."

"Backward?" Eva asked.

She reversed the reels and played it backward. A few seconds later they heard the chief sound man's voice. "Hi Sam, this is the Loch Ness monster."

Eva burst out laughing.

"Gene's done that before," Sam said with a grin. "Sent me a message by recording backward."

Katy Bear was a little disappointed it was not a voice from the other world. She went to call her aunt to say that she had arrived safely.

Tripper and Sam watched as Eva tried out the sound effects of howling wind along with the shot of the Western Isles Hotel. It worked quite well.

"I just want to trim a little off the beginning," Eva said, and she ran the film back and forth a few times. Then she stopped it on a frame and leaned forward to make a yellow grease-pencil mark so she would know where to cut the shot.

Suddenly she pulled back and stared at the frame.

"Now that really *is* strange." Eva spoke in a quiet voice that gave Tripper chills. "Look at this."

In the frame of 35mm film was a spot of bright light. It was right above the stone wall on the ledge that jutted out over the bay.

"It doesn't make sense," Eva said. "It's only on a single frame."

"Maybe it's static electricity," Tripper suggested.

Eva shook her head. "It would appear on more than one frame. Thirty-five millimeter film goes through the camera gate at the rate of twenty-four frames a second."

Sam was puzzled. "I suppose a lab problem would show up on more than one frame, too."

Eva nodded. "I've never seen anything like this."

She pulled out a small section of the film from the sprockets and held it up to the light. She studied the frame again for almost a minute.

Then she shrugged. "Well, one frame won't make much difference." She wound the piece back onto the sprockets, made a grease-pencil mark on the next frame, and cut the shot there. "I'm sure there's an excellent reason."

Without wasting any more time, she hung the piece in the trims barrel.

"There's *always* a reason," she said.

DeDe Simone

"If you don't mind. . . ." The girl was looking accusingly at Tripper and speaking to her in a cool, distant voice. Tripper couldn't figure out what the girl was talking about.

"I said, 'If you don't mind. . . .'" The girl had light gray eyes and was staring at Tripper as if she thought Tripper was a complete idiot.

Tripper and Sam were waiting at the dock at Oban for the ferry that would take them to the Isle of Mull. For the past half hour they had been studying this girl and her twin sister. In fact, they had been studying the whole family, who was waiting ahead of them in line for the ferry.

Sam couldn't get over the amount of

luggage they had: ". . . over thirty pieces, not including the matching golf bags," he whispered to Tripper. Everyone in the family had a set of matching luggage, and it was the twin with the gray tweed luggage who was so impatient with Tripper.

"If you don't mind. . . ." The girl pointed to the camera bag on Tripper's shoulder.

"I don't know what you're talking about," Tripper finally burst out.

Sam nudged Tripper. "Your camera bag is back here," he said.

Tripper turned around and saw that her camera bag was lying next to Sam's tape recorder on the pier. She suddenly realized she had picked up the girl's camera bag by mistake. It surprised Tripper that some- one close to her age had the same camera bag. She'd gotten hers in Singapore and it was designed to go into every region of the world: the jungle, the desert — even the Arctic Circle. She'd seen only profes- sional photographers with the same camera bag.

Tripper had done a lot of photography. She was quite good. Her job on location was to photograph her father's film crew at work.

The girl took the camera bag and turned her back on Tripper. Tripper heard her say quite clearly to her sister, "Some people seem to be a bit slow."

The only difference Tripper could see between the twins was the way they wore their hair. The twin who had spoken to Tripper wore her dusty blonde hair parted in the middle and pulled back severely with a barrette. But her sister wore her blonde hair just like her mother's — short and waved carefully to look casual and windblown. All three wore red-tinted sunglasses on top of their heads, tucked carefully into their hair.

The twins and their mother were dressed exactly alike in dark blue A-line wraparound skirts, crisp yellow blouses, and flat-heeled yellow pumps. They each had a white cable-knit sweater draped over their shoulders.

The father was dressed in a plaid kilt.

"He's the first person we've seen in a kilt," Sam whispered to Tripper. "I expected everyone in Scotland to be wearing kilts."

"And he's not even a Scotsman," Tripper said. "He's an American."

The father also had a white cable-knit sweater draped over his shoulders.

The ferry docked and began taking on cars and passengers. Tripper and Sam had to wait quite awhile for the family to get all their luggage up onto the boat. A voice over the loudspeaker told them that all bags were to be placed in the center passageway of the ferry.

The father of the twins seemed very concerned that the family's luggage be together and lined up in a certain way.

Tripper took her camera out of her camera bag. "I'm going up on the deck to take some pictures," she told Sam. "Want to come?"

Sam grinned. "No," he said. "Let's go to the cafeteria first. All this sea air is making me hungry."

Tripper stared at him. "But we just got on the ferry."

"Oh come on, Tripper. We're not going to eat until very late. When we get to Mull, we still have to take this long bus ride to Tobermory Bay."

"Well, I'll meet you down in the cafeteria," Tripper said, and she went up on the deck.

Tripper loved boats and she enjoyed taking pictures of sea and sky. She usually photographed in black and white. All that interested her was light and shadow and the different shades of gray.

She had just framed the perfect picture, with the lifeboats in the foreground, when suddenly her view was blocked.

The twins had draped themselves over the rail right in front of Tripper.

"Could you please move a little?" Tripper called, but they didn't seem to notice.

"Hey!" she said.

The twin with the long hair — the one who had already spoken to Tripper — turned around and stared at her. "Excuse me?" she asked coldly.

"I just want to get this picture," Tripper said.

The girl's gray eyes narrowed. "Well, if you insist. . . ."

"Oh, come on, DeDe," the other one said. "Let's go inside," and they moved off across the deck.

Tripper took a few more pictures and went down to the cafeteria. To her surprise Sam was at the very end of the line.

"What happened?" she asked.

Sam shrugged. "I got into a conversation with one of the deckhands about the history of the Tobermory Galleon."

Sam had already done quite a lot of reading about the history of Mull and the Tobermory Galleon in the New York Public Library where his mother worked.

"Tripper, do you realize that they don't even know what caused that explosion in 1588?"

"Well, what do they think?" Tripper asked.

"Some people think it was this local chieftain Lachlan Maclean who ordered the ship to be blown up. He had provided the ship with food and water when they sought shelter from a storm in Tobermory Bay, but he felt he hadn't been paid properly. Then some people think it was his wife, who was jealous of the Spanish princess who was said to have been on board. But then others say it was the cats. . . ."

"The cats?" Tripper asked.

"Yup. They say the Witch of Mull called up an army of fairy cats, who swam out to the Galleon and attacked the crew. It was the sparks off their fur that ignited the gunpowder!"

Tripper laughed. "I like that theory the best."

It was late afternoon and most of the people seemed to be drinking tea, but when their turn came, Tripper and Sam both ordered fish and chips.

There was one large table where no one was sitting, so they sat down and began to eat. A few minutes later the father of the twins sat down at the same table. The twins and their mother were standing in the aisle looking around. It was clear they were trying to find another table — a table where the family could be alone.

Finally they gave up and sat down with Tripper and Sam, without so much as glancing at them. Everyone in the family had a container of yogurt.

Tripper noticed that the twins ate their yogurt very methodically. First they skimmed a little off the top and slid the yogurt delicately into their mouths. Then they scraped the sides very evenly and neatly — another thin layer off the top. . . . Tripper wondered if it was fair to judge people by the way they ate yogurt.

Suddenly the mother turned to Sam and said, with a smile fixed upon her face, "And will you be staying over on the Isle of Mull?"

Sam nodded. "We're going to be staying at the Western Isles Hotel."

"That's where we've been staying! We just took a side trip to Edinburgh for a few days, but we kept our rooms at the hotel. You see, Lloyd is shopping for antique golf clubs. Golf clubs are his absolute passion. . . ."

The mother introduced herself as Missy Simone, ". . . but call me Missy." The twins, whose names turned out to be DeDe and Phyllis, sat there eating their yogurt and looking bored to death.

"Now, I spent *my* time in Edinburgh dabbling about with history — I simply adore that sort of thing." The mother's smile remained fixed on her face. "And DeDe had quite an exciting time being interviewed by all those newspapers about her latest photograph."

Tripper was interested. She turned to DeDe. "What sort of photography do you do?"

DeDe did not even look up from her yogurt. "I'd rather not talk about it right now, if you don't mind," she said.

Her mother looked very uncomfortable. Her father cleared his throat. "You might call DeDe's photographs *experimental*."

"Scientific," DeDe snapped.

"Phyllis, darling," the mother said to the twin, "would you mind terribly running out and getting DeDe's portfolio?"

Tripper noticed that DeDe did not object.

Phyllis groaned. "Do I have to?" she whined.

But she got to her feet and went out to get it. Tripper had the feeling that DeDe and Phyllis were used to being waited on at home. She was sure they were always being driven places and picked up by servants.

The father looked at Tripper's camera, which was lying on the table. "That's quite a fine piece of equipment," he said. "What sort of pictures do you take?"

Tripper had done all sorts of photography, but she just said, "I like to take pictures of people at work."

DeDe's eyes flickered over Tripper without interest. "That doesn't sound very artistic."

Tripper was annoyed, but at the same

time she was curious to see DeDe's work. When Phyllis returned with the portfolio, the mother took out an 8 x 10 black-and-white photograph and handed it to Sam to look at first. "This is DeDe's most recent work," she said.

Sam looked at the photo and blinked. Then he bent his head down and ran his fingers through his reddish-gold curls. Tripper had a feeling he was trying to hide a smile. But it was hard to tell with Sam. He had a wide, thin mouth that was always slightly turned up at the corners whether he was smiling or not.

When he finally spoke, he spoke in a low, serious voice. "Um . . . now where did you say this photograph was taken?" Tripper detected a slight squeak at the end. She was afraid Sam was going to burst out laughing.

"Right in front of the Western Isles Hotel," the father said. "My wife has an interesting theory about that." He turned to her. "Missy, tell them that little tidbit of information you picked up while you were doing that research in Edinburgh."

The mother seemed quite pleased with herself. "Well, it's right on the spot where the Macleans fired upon an early salvage operation on the Tobermory Galleon — in 1678, I believe."

"Why would they do that?" Tripper asked.

Sam turned to Tripper. "The Macleans have always felt they owned the rights to that wreck. But the Crown granted the rights to the Duke of Argyll, who was a Campbell. The Campbells were the traditional enemies of the Macleans."

"You have to understand," Missy Simone went on, "that DeDe is terribly sensitive to spirits. In fact she mentioned an 'encounter' only a few days before on the ledge right in front of that wall. Now, my hunch is that somehow she has recorded the ghost of one of those early Macleans. It may even be the ghost of Lachlan Maclean."

"I see," Sam said slowly, but with that same squeak in his voice, "and your theory is that the Macleans are getting . . . um . . . restless again because the Duke of Argyll — the present Duke of Argyll — has begun another salvage attempt on the Tobermory Galleon. . . ."

The father broke in. "Well, I must say I

was skeptical at first," he said, "but this photograph makes me understand why people say there are more kinds of life in this world than *life as we know it*."

"You mean, life as we *don't* know it?" Sam asked innocently.

Tripper saw DeDe glance quickly at Sam, but her father just nodded thoughtfully and said, "Now that's an excellent way of putting it."

Sam handed the photograph to Tripper, who took one look at it and said politely, "It's quite a nice photograph. Too bad you had something on your lens."

Tripper heard Sam make a spluttering sound and she looked up. Sam had his face turned away, but his shoulders were shaking with laughter.

Tripper looked around. The entire Simone family was staring at her in dead silence. She had obviously said the wrong thing.

It was a photograph, taken in the evening, of the stone wall on the ledge that jutted out over Tobermory Bay. Tripper had already seen that stone wall in the film footage she had seen of the Western Isles Hotel. In the darkness, right above the stone wall, was a foggy shape. Everything else in the photograph was clear.

It did seem a bit strange to Tripper that the blur had taken on such a definite shape, almost like a wisp of smoke or a figure.

She looked at DeDe. DeDe's face was in shadow, but she was watching Tripper out of the corner of her eye. In that light DeDe's eyes looked more violet than gray.

Tripper looked at the photograph again. There was something else about it that disturbed her.

All at once she realized what it was. The strange blurred shape was right above the old stone wall. It was in exactly the same place as the bright spot of light that had appeared on the single frame of film — the spot that had so mystified Eva.

Duart!

Tripper handed the photo back to Missy Simone, who was now chatting nervously about the Western Isles Hotel.

". . . a charming place full of Old World flavor. Of course I nearly died when I heard a film crew was staying there. You know how film people can be. Well, it turned out to be the documentary film director, Roger Tripper, who's terribly well-known and a perfectly lovely person."

When Missy Simone found out that Tripper was Roger Tripper's daughter, she was very impressed. Even the twins showed a slight interest in Tripper, but when they found out that Sam actually worked on the film crew, they turned all their attention on him.

Phyllis gave him a big smile. She smiled

just the way her mother smiled. "You know, you look so familiar to me. Have we met someplace before?"

"I don't think so," Sam said.

DeDe leaned across the table and said, "Gene must be a wonderful person to work with."

"Do you know Gene?" Sam asked.

DeDe didn't answer, but lowered her voice and said, "What do you think about all those weird things that have been happening on the production?"

"What weird things?" Sam asked.

DeDe looked at him in surprise. "Don't you know?" She gave her sister a meaningful look. "Well, Coco was saying — "

"You've met Coco?" Tripper was surprised that DeDe knew her father's electrician.

DeDe glanced briefly at Tripper. "Actually we've become quite close," she said, and turned back to Sam. "Coco is one of my favorite people. I'm so happy for her. You *do* know about her and Garrett."

"Who's Garrett?" Tripper asked.

DeDe raised her eyebrows. "The head diver on the salvage operation, of course. They're very much in love."

"I like John." Phyllis began talking about the grip on the film crew who did all the carpentry that was needed on the set. "He has a wonderful sense of humor even though he's terribly shy. . . ."

Tripper couldn't believe it. The Simone twins were talking about her father's film crew as if they had known them all their lives. Tripper was beginning to suspect they were just dropping names — that they had been hanging around the film crew, picking up gossip and film talk.

Tripper couldn't stand it another minute.

"Well, what *has* been happening on the production?" she asked. "What happened that was so weird?"

DeDe stopped talking and looked at Tripper. "Well, I'm afraid if you don't already know, I'd probably better not say anything."

Tripper was furious. She turned and saw Phyllis smiling at her with that fixed smile.

"I love your ring," Phyllis said. "Where did you get it?"

Tripper always wore a ring that had belonged to her mother. It was a strange cluster of opals and sapphires that had been given to her mother by the government of Thailand.

"Where did you get it?" Phyllis asked again.

"It belonged to my mother," Tripper said.

"Is she deceased?" DeDe asked with no emotion in her voice.

Sam was watching Tripper. He knew Tripper did not like to talk about her mother.

"Is she deceased?" DeDe asked again, staring at the ring.

"She died a long time ago," Sam said quietly.

Just then an announcement came over the loudspeaker of the ferry: "In a few minutes we will be able to see Duart Castle on the Isle of Mull. The castle dates from the thirteenth century and is the ancient stronghold of the Macleans of Duart, who succeeded the MacDonalds, Lords of the Isles, as the most powerful clan in the Southern Hebrides. Duart Castle is still the home of Lord and Lady Maclean and is open to the public. . . ."

"You simply must take the tour of that

castle," Missy Simone told Tripper and Sam. "Of course they claim there has never been a ghost at Duart, but DeDe felt a definite presence. . . ."

Tripper and Sam looked at each other. "I think I'll go up on deck and take some pictures," Tripper said.

"I'm coming, too." Sam stood up and they both left the cafeteria.

"I can't stand listening to any more of that spirit stuff," Sam said. They had stopped in the center passageway, where all the bags were stored, so that Tripper could pick up another roll of film. "I just can't see a bunch of ghosts going around posing for pictures. I'm sure they have better things to do — rattling chains, moaning and wailing, flitting about. . . ."

Tripper didn't smile. She had a fluttery feeling in her stomach. "But Sam, did you notice that the blurry figure in DeDe's photograph is in exactly the same place as that spot of light in the footage we saw in the cutting room — in the footage of the Western Isles Hotel?"

Sam nodded.

"Well, how do you explain that?" Tripper asked.

"Coincidence," Sam said abruptly, and he picked up his tape recorder. "I'm going to do some recording. Eva gave me a list of more wild sound she needs — seabirds, the sound of the ferry docking. . . ."

When they got up to the deck, the voice on the loudspeaker was saying: "If you look to the left, you will see, midway in the channel, a rock that has become known as Lady's Rock. At high tide this rock is covered by water and is considered most dangerous by sailors. The story goes that Lachlan Maclean wanted to get rid of his wife, who was the daughter of Lady Elisabeth Campbell and the Duke of Argyll. One night, it is said, he tied her up, rowed her out to the rock, and left her there, leaving the tide to do the rest. The next morning he looked out from Duart Castle and saw the rock swept bare. You can imagine his surprise when his wife appeared at the banquet table that evening. She had been rescued by a fisherman who was passing by. . . ."

Sam said, "I wonder if that was the same Lachlan Maclean who was accused of having blown up the Tobermory Galleon."

A tall gentleman in a tweed jacket turned around and smiled at both of them. "No," he said. "That was almost fifty years earlier. It was another Lachlan Maclean."

"Is it true?" Tripper asked. "Did he really do that to his wife?"

"Well, it makes a good story," the gentleman said dryly.

Just at that moment Duart Castle came into view.

Tripper caught her breath.

The castle stood on a great mass of rocks above the Sound of Mull. It stood alone on a peninsula outlined by the gray clouds overhead. The clouds were moving quickly across the sky.

What amazed Tripper was the way the light kept changing every few seconds on the castle and the ground surrounding it. There seemed to be both rain and sunshine up ahead.

Tripper began snapping pictures, trying to catch the light as it changed the shape of the landscape.

The gentleman in the tweed jacket was watching her photograph. Every once in a while he'd ask her a question or two about her photography. He was surprised to learn that she was using black-and-white film and that she did her own developing.

"I always carry my darkroom supplies with me," Tripper explained, "but I can only develop the negatives when I travel, unless I can find a darkroom someplace to print the pictures."

"There's a man named David Mac-Kinnon in Tobermory who has a darkroom — hasn't used it for years. He runs a bed and breakfast place and I'm sure he would be delighted to have you use it," the man told her.

Tripper thanked him for the information and took another series of shots of Duart Castle.

"Well, I'd better go down and see to the car," the gentleman said. "We'll be docking shortly. I certainly would like to see those photographs when you have prints. If you're in the neighborhood of Craignure, please stop by."

When Tripper turned around, the man was gone.

"Sam," Tripper said. "That was odd.

That man said he wanted to see my photographs and he invited me to stop by when I was in the neighborhood, but he didn't even tell me his name."

"Who?" Sam asked.

"That man. The man I was just talking to."

Sam looked blank. "I didn't see you talking to anyone," he said.

"What do you mean? Just now." Tripper had that fluttery feeling again. "He was standing right here!"

"Oh really?" Sam seemed very puzzled. "You mean there was a mysterious stranger, who just disappeared into thin air?"

Tripper stared at Sam. "Hold on just a minute," she said. "You talked to him, too. You asked about Lachlan Maclean."

All at once she realized Sam was teasing her. "You did see him, didn't you?"

Sam grinned. "Sorry, Tripper. I couldn't help it. Do you know the poem:

> As I was climbing up the stair
> I met a man who wasn't there.
> He wasn't there again today.
> Oh, how I wish he'd go away."

"Sam," Tripper said. "I'll get you back for that."

Sam laughed.

Sam went to the bow of the ferry to do some recording. Tripper rewound her film and tucked the roll into her pocket.

Then she stood on the deck gazing at the mist-covered hills in the distance and the sea lochs that wound in and out along the coast of Mull. She looked up and saw a perfect rainbow stretched across the sky. Its brilliant colors almost looked as if they had been painted on the dark, silvery-gray clouds.

Tripper felt she was coming to a magic island — a timeless place — a setting for a fairy tale.

The Mysterious
Stranger

As soon as the ferry pulled into the dock at Craignure, the sky turned dark and it began to rain. There was a bus marked TOBERMORY, standing at the end of the pier.

Tripper and Sam had to wait for the Simone family to get all their luggage into the compartments under the bus.

"I wonder if we should take our rain jackets out of our bags," Tripper said.

Just then Phyllis wailed, "My mirror combination case! I don't see my mirror combination case!" and she made the bus driver go through all the luggage in the compartment under the bus.

The rest of the Simone family had already gotten onto the bus and was saving a seat for her.

"Hurry up, Phyllis," her mother called

out the window. "We want to make sure we have our seats all together."

"But my mirror combination case isn't here," Phyllis called.

Tripper and Sam were getting very wet. "What is a mirror combination case?" Sam muttered.

"I'll bet it's one of those mirrors with lights around it and stuff that makes steam. . . ."

They saw Missy Simone climb down from the bus and put up a large black umbrella. She made the bus driver go through all the luggage again.

"Oh dear," she said. "It must still be on the ferry." She turned around and noticed Sam. "Would you mind terribly? . . ."

Sam looked at Tripper. "Say no," Tripper murmured, but she knew it would be hard for him to refuse.

Sam shrugged. "I'll go have a look," he said. He turned to Tripper. "Keep an eye on the sound equipment," he told her. "Don't put it in the luggage compartment. I'd rather carry it aboard."

Tripper placed her camera bag next to the metal case with Sam's tape recorder and microphone in it. Then she tried to squeeze their other bags into the compartment under the bus.

"Oh here it is," she heard Phyllis say. "It was all mixed in with someone else's stuff."

Tripper turned around in time to see Phyllis and her mother climbing back onto the bus.

"Wait a minute!" Tripper called. "You have to tell Sam."

But they didn't even turn around.

Tripper stood there a moment, trying to figure out what to do. The metal case with the sound equipment was quite heavy, but she picked it up along with her camera case and struggled through the pouring rain to the ferry ramp.

A deckhand waved down to her. "Don't worry, lassie," he called. "Your friend will be right down."

Sam came down the ramp. He was soaking wet. "It's not there," he said. "I looked all over."

"I know," Tripper said. "Phyllis found it."

Sam took the metal case from Tripper and they hurried to the end of the pier.

The bus was gone.

"Oh no!" Tripper said. "Now we have to wait for the next bus. And our bags are on that one. You would have thought someone in that Simone family would have said something to the bus driver. That is the most self-centered family I have ever met."

"I'll try to find out what time the next bus leaves," Sam said.

But there were no signs and there were no people on the pier to ask.

The last car was driving off the ferry. Sam waved to the driver, who slowed down and stopped.

Tripper watched Sam run over to the car and shake hands with the driver. It was the gentleman in the tweed jacket — "the mysterious stranger."

"Hurry up, Sam," Tripper muttered. She was drenched.

Just then Sam signaled to her. "Come on, Tripper," he called.

"But. . . ."

Sam was already climbing into the front seat. Tripper hesitated. Sam turned around. "Hurry up, Tripper. Get in the car!"

She figured Sam must know what he was doing, so she climbed into the backseat.

The man turned on the motor and the windshield wipers and they took off through the driving rain.

"Where are we going?" she asked as he turned left off the pier. (Tripper was pretty sure Tobermory was to the right.)

"We have to get to a telephone and call your father," Sam said.

"And try to find you a ride to Tobermory tonight. But I'm afraid it won't be easy," the mysterious stranger said.

"That's all right," Tripper said nervously. "We'll just take the next bus."

"There is no next bus," Sam told her. "No bus until tomorrow."

Tripper was quiet. She tried to see through the rain beating against the windshield of the car. They were on a deserted road. There were no houses. The landscape seemed wild and savage. All Tripper could see were heather and gorse bushes blown flat by the heavy gusts of wind.

"Are we almost at the town?" she asked, trying to keep her voice steady.

"We passed that long ago," the mysterious stranger said. "Craignure isn't much of a town — just a post office, a store or two — but it's all closed up by now. This part of Mull is not very inhabited."

For no reason at all, Tripper found herself thinking of a line from one of Katy Bear's favorite gothic novels, which was called *Ghastly Moonlight*. "His face was like a mask." The line kept repeating itself over and over in Tripper's head in time to the steady beat of the windshield wipers: "His face was like a mask. His face was like a. . . ."

Tripper tried to catch a glimpse of the mysterious stranger's face in the rearview mirror.

But suddenly the man stopped the car right in the middle of the lonely road and began backing up quickly.

"What are you doing?" Tripper could not keep the panic out of her voice. She thought the man was behaving very strangely.

"Shh, Tripper," Sam said. "Take it easy. This is a one-track road. We have to yield to that car."

"What car?" Tripper asked suspiciously and peered through the windshield.

"Didn't you see the headlights?" Sam asked.

"No," Tripper said.

"Well, they must have disappeared on the other side of the hill. We'll see them again in a minute."

The man backed the car into a small clearing at the side of the road and stopped.

"I hope no one's been telling you stories of these ghost cars," the mysterious stranger said as they waited. "Those stories are very popular on these islands."

"You mean headlights appear in the distance. You wait, but the car never comes?" Sam asked.

The man nodded.

Tripper held her breath. To her relief, the headlights of a car finally appeared over the top of the hill and a minute later the car passed them, honking its horn in thanks.

Once again they were driving through the darkness and rain. Tripper found herself composing a postcard to Katy Bear: *Here we are driving on a lonely deserted road with a mysterious stranger. It is a wild and stormy night. . . .*

Suddenly the man turned off onto an even smaller road. They were climbing a steep hill.

"We're almost there," Sam said.

Looming up ahead of them in the darkness Tripper saw a great mass of building.

"Duart Castle?" she asked.

It was at that point that Tripper decided things had gone far enough.

"Look," she said to the mysterious stranger. "All we want is a telephone so I can call my father. This is not exactly the time for sightseeing. . . ."

"Sightseeing?" Sam turned around. When he saw the expression on Tripper's face, he suddenly understood.

"Tripper," Sam said. "I'd like you to meet Lord Maclean."

In the Dead
of Night

Dear Katy Bear,

It is a wild and stormy night. My hand trembles as I write this letter. Something has occurred that fills me with the deepest and darkest dread. . . .

Ha! I just thought that was a good beginning for a letter from the 13th century castle. As a matter of fact I feel quite cozy and at home at Duart Castle, where Sam and I are spending the night.

Sam is sleeping across the Public Courtyard in the living quarters. There are 100 rooms there, but, believe it or not, every

49

room is filled tonight. You see, there is a gathering of the clan, and Lord and Lady Maclean are very busy attending to all their guests. There was no room for me in that part of the castle so I get to sleep in the State Bedroom!

The State Bedroom is in the old part of the castle. It is part of a museum during the day and is open to the public. It is a beautiful room with a desk that once belonged to the poet William Wordsworth. There is a big fourposter bed with a canopy, a beautiful settee, and the most enormous wardrobe chest you have ever seen — almost as big as a room.

Before I retired for the night, a very nice maid brought me a cup of cocoa. (You know how fussy I am about getting a decent cup of cocoa.) It was the best cocoa I have ever had. The recipe, she told me, comes from the Isle of Mull chocolate factory and is made with melted chocolate, egg, and whipped cream. It was delicious.

You will probably be very disappointed to learn that there are no ghosts here at Duart Castle. Lord Maclean did his best to find us something, and asked us if mysterious dog paw prints would do. Then he took us up a circular stone staircase that leads to the ramparts. On one step there was a dog paw print in the cement. It had appeared, he told us, when new cement was put in, but no one knows how it got there.

I'm afraid Sam and I didn't look too impressed, because he apologized for the lack of ghosts. He then asked me if I would care to develop the negatives of Duart Castle I shot on the ferry. I told him I needed a darkroom, and he offered me the dungeon. I have a feeling he might have been joking, but I said, "Fine."

Right now my negatives are hanging to dry in the dungeon. I hope the photographs will be good. I haven't had a chance to get a good look at the negatives yet, but I think a set of nice black-and-white prints of Duart Castle would make a very good thank-you present for Lord and Lady Maclean.

Lord Maclean has already met my father. In fact the film crew was here, shooting a sequence of the castle. My father will pick us up very early tomorrow morning.

The rain has stopped. I feel quite sleepy so I will finish this letter tomorrow. . . .

Tripper changed into the big soft night-gown that had been put out for her. She turned off the lamp and climbed into the big fourposter bed. She wished she didn't feel so sleepy. It seemed such a waste of time to sleep when she was spending the night at a real castle.

She was just drifting off to sleep when she heard, somewhere below her, a creaking sound. It sounded as if one of the enormous doors to the Banquet Room was opening very slowly. But she knew sound traveled in strange ways in a castle like this, especially since some of the walls were ten feet thick.

A few minutes later she heard the creaking again.

"Old castles are creaky," she told herself and she pulled the covers up. In no time at all she was asleep.

Suddenly she woke up. She had been dreaming about the suit of armor she had seen downstairs in the museum. In her dream the face mask kept opening and closing. Just at that moment she heard the squeak of old metal opening and closing.

Tripper tried to remember the floor plan of the old part of the castle and where exactly she had seen that suit of armor. She lay in bed waiting and, once again, she heard the squeaking of the hinges opening and closing.

Tripper threw off the covers and turned on the lamp. She looked around. There were small windows set into the thick stone walls of the State Bedroom. She crawled into one of the recesses and looked out.

She could see the Public Courtyard between the old castle and the living quarters across the way. On the side of the courtyard was a rowan tree — a tree that had been planted to ward off witches and evil spirts. She tried to figure out an Escape Plan just in case she got frightened.

For, at that moment, Tripper did not feel frightened. And she was sure it was just her imagination that made her think she heard hushed whispers floating through the stone stairways of the ancient castle.

Everything was quiet so she turned off the light and got back into bed. She closed her eyes.

It was then that she heard the rattle of a chain being dragged across a wooden surface — slow and deliberate. The sound came from somewhere below her and went on for a few seconds.

Tripper lay in bed trying to be fair to ghosts. "Ghosts," Tripper told herself, "have just as much right to be here as I do. More right, I suppose, since I am just a visitor. It is a question of respecting one another's rights. . . ."

Once again she heard the dreadful sound of the chain being dragged across a dull wooden surface. Very slowly — link by link. . . .

"Hello . . . test. Hello . . . test." Sam adjusted his headphones and spoke in a hushed voice into the smaller microphone he used to slate sound effects. "The next sound will be the sound of anchor chains on a wooden boat."

Sam looked up and nodded to Lord Maclean, who was standing silently by the edge of a table near the other microphone that was on a stand.

Very slowly Lord Maclean dragged the small chain over the edge of the heavy wooden table. He seemed to be enjoying helping Sam record some of the sound effects Eva had requested. They were working on the list of Harbor Sounds. They had already done all the sound effects needed for the sequence that had been shot at Duart Castle.

Lord Maclean had found a creaky box made of banana wood, which had served very well as the creaking door.

Sam handed Lord Maclean a set of headphones and played back the tape of the chain rattling across the table. Lord Maclean listened to it and nodded.

Sam picked up the microphone stand and his tape recorder and they both quietly slipped into the outer room, which was called the Sea Room.

"You see," Sam said in a quiet voice, "it's very important to record sound effects when the background is as quiet as possible. That's why it's best to record them in the middle of the night. It is also important that the sound not be exaggerated. The actual sound of an anchor chain being dragged across the deck of a wooden boat might not sound as good as that small chain."

Sam looked over Eva's shot list of sound effects. He checked off CREAKING DOOR: DUART CASTLE; FACE MASK ON SUIT OF

ARMOR OPENING AND CLOSING: DUART CASTLE. . . . Then he looked over the list of Harbor Sounds. There didn't seem to be anything else they could take care of that evening until Sam noticed HARBOR SOUNDS: FLOCK OF BIRDS TAKING OFF.

"By the way," Sam said. "There is a way of doing that without any birds at all. It might be fun to try. . . ."

Once again Tripper heard those strange hushed whispers floating up the stone staircase and she decided she was now ready to carry out her Escape Plan. She found her camera case next to the bed, reached in, and took out her flashlight. She went to the window to review the route.

She looked down into the darkness of the Public Courtyard. A few feet away from the rowan tree she saw a white sheet flapping violently in midair!

"Well, it certainly does sound like a flock of birds." Lord Maclean took off the headphones and handed them back to Sam.

"It sounds more like a flock of birds than a flock of birds," Sam said.

Lord Maclean told Sam what fun it had been and excused himself.

Sam began packing up. He closed the tape recorder and logged in the tape: WILD SOUND: FLOCK OF BIRDS TAKING OFF.

It was very still now in the courtyard. Luckily there had been very little wind when they had been shaking the sheet up and down to imitate a flock of birds.

Sam found himself hoping that the rowan tree was doing a good job of warding off evil spirits.

As he was taking down the stand for the microphone, he happened to look up and see, in one of the windows in the old part of the castle, a strange green light.

Sam froze. The light disappeared. A few seconds later, however, it appeared in another small window, and then another. . . .

When the green light appeared in the doorway to the Keep, on the ground floor, right across the courtyard from him, Sam held perfectly still and watched it. His voice didn't seem to be working.

Slowly the light moved out into the courtyard. It was heading right toward him. . . .

"Tripper," Sam said the next morning.

"You scared the life out of me. That green light of yours was the eeriest thing I have ever seen."

"Well, I never thought of taking the green filter off my flashlight. Sam, you know I always use that filter when I'm developing negatives. I can see how they're coming up, but the green light won't affect them. Otherwise I'd have to do it in total darkness."

Tripper and Sam were waiting in the Visitor's Tea Room of Duart Castle. Her father was coming very early to pick them up and take them to Tobermory Bay. They had eaten some delicious home-baked bran scones, but they tried not to eat too many. They would be having a large Scottish breakfast when they got to the Western Isles Hotel.

Lord Maclean stopped by the Visitor's Tea Room to say good-bye.

Tripper thanked him for his and Lady Maclean's hospitality. In a burst of enthusiasm and gratitude she added, ". . . and I just want you to know that I am sure your ancestor Lachlan Maclean was a very sweet person and had absolutely nothing to do with the explosion of the Tobermory Galleon."

"Well. . . ." Lord Maclean seemed to find that very amusing.

When he had gone, Sam said, "Tripper, you know it is highly likely that Lachlan Maclean *was* involved in some way with that explosion."

But, by now, Tripper would not hear any gossip about any relative of Lord Maclean no matter how long ago he had lived.

"You have no proof," Tripper told Sam. "And even if he did have something to do with it, he probably had a very good reason. Didn't you tell me he felt he hadn't been paid properly for providing the Galleon with food and water?"

"Well," Sam said. "He was actually given a band of Spanish soldiers from the ship. He used them to attack neighboring islands and massacre the families there. I read a report that said the Spanish soldiers returned completely dazed from the expedition. They had never seen anything like the bloodshed that went along with this type of clan warfare in the Western Highlands."

"You mean chopping off heads and things like that?" Tripper asked.

Sam nodded.

Tripper thought about that. "Well, if he wasn't out chopping off *their* heads, they might have been on Mull chopping off *his* family's heads."

"There's some truth to that," Sam said. "But then there was the time Lachlan Maclean's mother remarried and Lachlan is said to have murdered eighteen of her wedding guests."

"Temper tantrum," Tripper said abruptly. "I'm sure he was sorry afterward." Then she grinned at Sam. "No one is picking on Lachlan Maclean," she said.

Tripper remembered her negatives hanging in the dungeon and went to get them.

"How are they?" Sam asked Tripper when she returned.

"I haven't had a good look at them yet," Tripper said. She took them out of the glassine envelope and went over to the window. She held them up to the daylight.

Sam watched Tripper move a row of negatives slowly up and down. He had often seen Tripper "read" negatives, as she called it. He knew that, in a certain light, the negatives looked positive and were much easier to see.

Tripper seemed disturbed about something. She walked over to the table, reached into her camera bag, and took out a small magnifying glass. Once again she took the negatives to the window and looked at them one by one with the magnifying glass.

"What's the matter?" Sam asked.

Tripper didn't answer.

"Aren't you going to show them to Lord Maclean?" Sam asked her.

Tripper returned to the table. She stuck the negatives carefully into the glassine envelope. She sat down.

"Sam," she said quietly, "I will never show these negatives to anyone."

"What's wrong?" Sam asked. "The exposure?"

Tripper shook her head. "The exposure is fine," she said. Her voice was trembling. "I've got to look at them under an enlarger."

"What's wrong with them?" Sam asked.

Tripper was staring into space. She seemed completely bewildered.

Sam shook her arm gently. "Tripper," he said. "What's the matter?"

"I took those photographs," Tripper said in a dull voice. "I took those photographs."

"Yes," Sam said. "I know. Look, Tripper, if they didn't turn out, you can always shoot them again. You can take more pictures on the ferry on the way back. Maybe we can even make a special trip to Oban. Oh, I know you're going to say that the light will be different, but. . . ."

Sam stopped and looked at Tripper. It wasn't like her to take things this seriously. But then again, she didn't often make mistakes with her photography.

"Oh, come on, Tripper. Everyone messes up once in a while," Sam said. "What was it — the focus? It was the focus, wasn't it?"

"The focus is perfect," Tripper snapped. "Everything is sharp and clear — the castle, the water in the Sound of Mull, the clouds, the face in the clouds. . . ."

Tripper covered her eyes with her hands.

"The face is in perfect focus."

"What face?" Sam asked.

"The face in the clouds over Duart Castle," Tripper whispered. "The face looking out from the clouds."

"But whose face is it?"

"I don't know." Tripper was almost in tears. "It looks like the face of some wild Scotsman — it's a face from another century!"

"May I have a look?" Sam asked.

Tripper shrugged and handed Sam the negatives.

He took them out of the glassine envelope and held them up to the light. He studied them one by one. Then he tucked them back into the envelope and handed them to Tripper. "Well, at least we know who it is."

"What do you mean?" Tripper asked.

"It's the same face that was in the portrait in the Banquet Hall," Sam said. He seemed quite puzzled.

"What face?" Tripper asked. "I didn't look at any of those portraits. I don't know which one you're talking about."

"The one of Lachlan Maclean," Sam said. "It's the face of Lachlan Maclean."

A Scottish Breakfast

The minute Tripper caught sight of the town of Tobermory, she felt better. She lost the sense of uneasiness she had had all during the drive from Duart Castle, thinking about those negatives.

The town seemed so real — so down-to-earth. It was a beautiful fishing village with brightly colored buildings and shops in a row along the waterfront. Stone quays covered with bright orange fishing nets jutted out into the bay. There was a big clock tower right in the center of town and a small seafood stand next to it.

When they arrived at the Western Isles Hotel, they saw the film crew setting up to shoot on the ledge overlooking the harbor. Tripper immediately recognized the semicircular stone wall that had appeared in the film footage of the Western Isles and in DeDe's photograph — on the ledge DeDe claimed was haunted.

"We're filming an interview this morning," Roger Tripper told them. "The dive has been called off today. Trouble with the big pumps. We're going to shoot the interview on the ledge with the harbor and boats in the background."

Everyone on the film crew was happy to see Tripper and Sam. Coco, the electrician, hugged both of them. Gene wanted to talk to Sam right away, but not about sound recording; he wanted to know if Sam wanted to go fishing with him that afternoon. Nick, the cameraman, was busy, but he winked at Tripper. John, the grip who did all the carpentry on the set, mumbled a shy hello.

"Where are Carlos and Leroy?" Tripper asked. Carlos was the assistant cameraman and Leroy was the unit manager.

"They went down to London," her father told her. "We had equipment problems. The casing on one of the underwater cameras sprang a leak, so it had to be repaired."

"Dad, has anything strange happened

on the production — anything *weird*?"

"Not at all." Roger Tripper smiled. "Just the usual things — some equipment troubles and now this delay with the pumps."

Tripper took her camera bag up to her room. Her other bags were already there. It was a lovely room — a gable room that looked out on the bay. The wallpaper had buttercups on it and there was a small tea table by the door. Tripper washed up and changed her clothes. She decided not to unpack; she was too hungry.

On the way down to breakfast, she suddenly stopped on the dark, winding staircase. She had a funny feeling she was being watched. She stood for a moment, poised on the staircase, her hand on the dark wooden banister.

There was sunlight coming down through the window on the landing above, but the landing below was in shadow. Standing in the shadows of the hallway was a camera on a tripod. It was a Contax — one of the best cameras in the world.

Tripper noticed a cable release cord running from the camera along the floor and into the doorway of one of the rooms. The door was slightly open.

Tripper knew she wasn't being spied upon by a camera. Someone was watching her from behind that door. And she had a feeling it was DeDe Simone.

The Scottish breakfast gave Tripper an even stronger sense of reality. She had worked her way through fresh fruit cup, kippers, oatmeal porridge, eggs and bacon, sausages and tomato and oatcakes with preserves. She had also tasted some of the haggis that Sam seemed to be enjoying so much.

"This haggis is delicious," Sam said. "What *is* haggis, anyway?"

Roger Tripper looked down at Sam's plate. Then he turned and looked out the window of the hotel dining room. "I wonder when those pumps will be fixed. I spoke to the dive supervisor this morning and he's afraid they won't get in a repair team for a few days."

From the large bay windows of the Western Isles dining room, they could see the film crew setting up on the ledge, and beyond that, Tobermory Bay dotted with small sailboats and fishing boats.

Right in the middle of the bay — about 100 yards from the shore — were large barges with all the equipment for the diving operation. There were pumps to pump air from the surface through hoses to the divers' hard helmets and face masks. There were control boards for the engineers and decompression tanks.

But there were also enormous pumps that worked like giant vacuum cleaners. The pumps were used to suck mud and silt from the bottom. A large sieve worked like a strainer to sort out metal and other objects that might be of interest. But this morning the big pumps were silent.

"I can't get over it," Sam said. "There is a ship that has been buried under layers of mud and boulders for four hundred years — right in view of the town. And, in all this time, no one has found anything of any real importance."

"That's true," Roger Tripper said. "There have been a number of salvage dives, but all that's been found are a few small cannon, cannonballs, some coins, and other bits and pieces — a skull, some silverware. And yet, it was said to have been the pay ship of the entire Spanish fleet. Every kid in Scotland believes there are treasure chests of gold down there."

Sam took another helping of haggis. "What did you say haggis was?" he asked again.

Roger Tripper gazed thoughtfully at Sam's plate. Then he turned to Tripper. "You know, I've arranged for you to use a darkroom here on Mull. A very nice man named David MacKinnon said he would be more than happy for you to use his."

"I already have his name," Tripper said. "Lord Maclean told me he had a darkroom."

"David's a very interesting man," her father went on. "He's a retired detective; used to be with the Scottish Border Police. His specialty was using photographic evidence to solve crimes."

Tripper relaxed and took another blood sausage. She was sure that, once she looked at those negatives under an enlarger, she would understand how the face of a man who had lived 400 years ago got into those clouds above Duart Castle.

"However," her father went on, "I'm afraid you will have to share it with an American girl who's also staying here."

"DeDe Simone?" Tripper asked.

Her father nodded. "Have you already met her?"

"On the ferry," Tripper said, and she looked at Sam. "Does she know I'll be sharing the darkroom with her?"

Her father looked a little uncomfortable. "Well, apparently, when she found out last night, she threw a bit of a temper tantrum — said she couldn't bear to have her 'space invaded,' but David told her right away that she would either share it or not use it at all. None of the local residents are very happy about these 'spirit photographs' DeDe keeps turning out."

He turned and watched the film crew setting up. Suddenly he said, "What in the world is Coco doing? We don't need all those lights. She has four lights set up. All we need is one to cut the contrast."

Tripper looked and saw that Nick, the cameraman, seemed to be discussing those lights with Coco, too. "I think she's putting up a hair light," Tripper told her father. "And another light to bring out the sparkles in someone's eyes."

Her father laughed. "Of course!" he said. "Now I understand. This morning we will be interviewing Garrett, the head diver. Coco is turning him into a star. . . ."

Tripper remembered something else DeDe had said on the ferry. "Dad," she said, "are Coco and Garrett in love?"

Her father smiled. "I don't know. Everyone on Mull thinks so. But Coco has suddenly become very shy. Whenever Garrett speaks to her, she clams up or else she gets her words mixed up. Too bad. Garrett is one of the nicest people I have ever met."

"What are you going to ask him in the interview?" Sam asked.

Roger Tripper looked worried. "I don't know. Divers are sworn to absolute secrecy. In fact, they sign a paper before they are hired on a salvage operation like this. They have to promise not to say a word to anyone about what they find or don't find. I don't know what to ask him in the interview that he can talk about freely."

"Is that him?" Tripper asked. "Is that Garrett?"

The most handsome man Tripper had ever seen walked up to Coco and said something to her. Coco almost dropped the light she was holding. The man had blond hair and dark blue eyes that twinkled. He had a friendly, kind smile. Right behind him was a little boy.

"Who's the little boy?" Tripper asked.

"That's Toby," her father told her. "He's David MacKinnon's grandson. He follows Garrett all over town. Toby wants to be a diver when he grows up. Most of the kids in this town do."

They watched Toby. Everything that Garrett did, Toby did. He walked like Garrett, he stood like Garrett, and the rest of the time, he just stared wistfully up at the diver.

Roger Tripper laughed. "Toby keeps begging Garrett to leave some treasure down there for him to find when he's old enough to dive for it."

Sam said, "Maybe you could get Toby to do the interview. Have him ask Garrett how he became a diver. I'd be interested in how he was trained and how he makes a living as a diver. Maybe he wanted to be a diver when he was little, too."

Roger Tripper seemed pleased with the idea. He stood up. "You know, I think I'll go talk to those two about it."

As he was leaving the dining room, the Simone family walked in. Tripper saw Missy stop her father and say something to him. He nodded and then excused himself.

Once again, the twins and their mother were dressed exactly alike, but this morning it was pink A-line skirts, flowered blouses, and pink flat-heeled pumps. The father was wearing golf shorts instead of a kilt, but they all had their cable-knit sweaters draped over their shoulders.

Tripper noticed that DeDe looked quite pale. She had dark circles under her eyes. She looked as if she had not slept at all. Before she sat down at the table, she looked steadily at Tripper for a few seconds — with a look of cool hatred.

But Phyllis came over to them with a big smile.

"Where *were* you?" she asked. "We looked all over for you yesterday."

"Oh really?" Tripper asked sweetly. "And where did you look?"

"All over," Phyllis repeated. "All over the bus."

"And were we there?" Tripper asked. She felt Sam kick her under the table.

Phyllis looked at her blankly. "No, but. . . ." She turned to Sam. "Guess what. I found my mirror combination case."

Sam nodded.

"It was right on the bus," Phyllis said.

"But was anything *missing* from the bus?" Tripper asked.

"Tripper!" Sam said under his breath. "Cut it out."

Phyllis shrugged. Suddenly her mouth fell open. She was staring down at Sam's plate with a look of horror. "You're not eating haggis, are you?"

She backed away from their table and joined her family at the next one. "He's eating haggis," she told her family. "How *could* he?"

"What is haggis, anyway?" Sam whispered to Tripper. "Do *you* know?"

"Well," Tripper began. "Actually, I *do* know. . . ."

Just then Missy Simone gasped. She was staring out the window. "Not there!" she said. "They're not planning to film there!" She turned around and said to Tripper, "But that's the very place DeDe has had her *encounters*."

"I'm sure it will be all right," Tripper mumbled.

"Well, I was just telling your father that DeDe no longer feels the presence on the ledge is the ghost of Lachlan Maclean. She says it's not Lachlan Maclean at all."

"That's nice," Tripper said, and she checked to make sure her shoulder bag was still hanging on the back of her chair. She had put those negatives of Lachlan Maclean into the side pocket.

"No," Missy went on. "She is quite sure now that it is a female presence. I can't understand why your father doesn't want to include DeDe in this film he is making."

"Mother!" DeDe said crossly. "I don't want to talk about it."

"But darling," Missy said, "surely it must be the ghost of that Spanish princess who was aboard the Galleon — the one who had the dream." She turned to Tripper and

Sam. "You do know about that dream, don't you?"

Sam said, "I think I read something about it."

"Oh, it's terribly romantic!" Missy said. "You see, the daughter of the King of Spain had a dream. She fell in love with a man she saw in this dream and made up her mind to sail the seven seas in search of him. So she sailed aboard the Galleon trying to find this man who kept appearing in her dream. Finally, when they reached the Isle of Mull, she saw Lachlan Maclean and recognized the man she had seen in her dreams. Of course his wife got jealous — "

" — hired the witch, who hired the cats, and BOOM!" her husband finished.

"Well, in any case, Lloyd and I had a long talk this morning and we're quite sure the figure in the photograph is the daughter of the King of Spain."

Suddenly DeDe whirled around in her chair. Her eyes were blazing with anger. "Mother!" she said. "That is only a theory."

"Well, what are you going to tell the reporter this morning?" her mother asked. "He's coming all the way from Edinburgh to interview you for the *Psychic Times*."

DeDe didn't say anything for a few seconds. She turned her head and looked out the window. When she spoke, she spoke in a calm, dreamlike voice: "No, Mother," she said. "What frightened me last night was quite different. It happened right here on the stairway of the Western Isles. I felt a definite presence — a female presence — but it was not connected in any way with the Tobermory Galleon or with the figure on the ledge."

Tripper felt like giggling. So DeDe had set up her Contax on a tripod to catch still another unsuspecting ghost. It would be quite an expensive loss if the ghost happened to be a clumsy ghost and tripped over the tripod.

"Oh dear," Missy said. "And whose spirit was that?"

"Well," DeDe said slowly. "I had the strong feeling of a mother — a mother searching for a child."

DeDe turned around and looked thoughtfully at Tripper. Her eyes rested for a few seconds on Tripper's opal and sapphire ring — the one that had belonged to her mother.

Suddenly Tripper felt dizzy. She looked

at Sam and saw his eyes were flashing with anger. Tripper had a strange feeling she was engaged in a battle; she was under attack. But she was on unfamiliar ground. And she had no weapons with which to fight back.

She looked over at the Simones, who were all now eating their yogurt. They were eating in the same methodical way they had eaten yogurt the day before on the ferry from Oban — delicately scraping a thin layer off the top; daintily slipping the spoons into their mouths. . . .

"Sam," Tripper said suddenly in a rather loud voice. "How *are* you enjoying your *sheep's stomach*?"

She saw a shudder run through every member of the Simone family. DeDe dropped her spoon; she looked quite ill.

Sam looked startled for a moment. He looked down at the plate of haggis. But then he noticed the reaction of the Simone family. None of them seemed interested in eating any more yogurt.

"It's excellent," Sam said. "I am quite fond of *sheep's stomach*." He waited for another shudder to run through the members of the Simone family.

"But you know, Sam," Tripper went on, "*sheep's stomach* may be delicious, but I can't wait to taste those *sheep eyeballs.* It's a specialty in Scotland. . . ."

It wasn't much of a revenge, but it was better than nothing. . . .

Garrett

The interview that morning went extremely well. Toby's first question to Garrett wasn't exactly a question.

He leaned against the stone wall overlooking the bay and looked up at Garrett. He studied the diver for a few seconds. Then he said, "Well, I guess you must be thinking about eels."

Garrett grinned and said that he did, indeed, spend a certain amount of time thinking about eels. He didn't like them very much, "especially when I am diving dark. Sometimes you can't use a light at all. A light would reflect off the mud and silt. It would be even harder to see. You have to spend your time feeling around in the dark. I had a job like that diving for a wreck off the coast of Norway. . . ."

Toby listened to the story with great eagerness. Then he said to the camera, "It's those moray eels he doesn't like. They have these big strong jaws and, once they take a bite out of you, they can't let go with their teeth. You have to chop their heads off." He pointed over the stone wall. "There's one right over there lying off the Mishnish Pier. Now Iain will be telling you it's fifteen feet long, but it's only nine."

Garrett nodded. "Yes, I know about that one." He paused. "Is Iain one of your schoolmates?"

Toby said, "Yes, but he likes the Quiet Room and I like the Noisy Room."

The conversation between the little boy and the diver was lively and natural. It turned out that Garrett had always wanted to be a diver. He talked about his childhood and training. He was not from Mull. He was from a different part of Scotland — from the Lowlands.

Roger Tripper was pleased. The film audience would learn a lot about diving from this interview, and they would also learn about the life of a little boy on the Isle of Mull and his dreams of diving for treasure.

Sam and Gene were having trouble with

the sound recording. Gene was sitting back at the mixer and Sam went over to talk to him a few times.

The trouble was that Garrett spoke in a low, gentle voice, as did most of the Scots they had met so far. Sam did some adjusting of the microphones that were placed under Garrett's and Toby's necks. Finally Gene and Sam decided to use a boom mike in addition to the other mikes, so that the sound would have more depth. It seemed to work.

But the next take was interrupted by the loud voices of the Simone family, who were on the steps leading down from the hotel.

"I still think a day on the golf course would do her good," they heard Lloyd Simone say.

"But darling, DeDe is upset about something. Terribly upset. She even canceled her interview with that reporter. She wants to spend the morning in the darkroom. And I think it's best if we let her do that."

The film crew had to wait until their voices faded away.

Tripper looked up and saw DeDe watching them from one of the windows of the hotel. A few minutes later, she appeared on the ledge and took some pictures of Garrett. Before she left, she said to Tripper, "Oh, by the way, I will be using the darkroom for a while. I'm sure your snapshots can wait."

Tripper watched her go off. It was then that she noticed that a small crowd had gathered to watch the filming. Roger Tripper usually didn't mind if people watched as long as they were quiet and stayed out of the way.

But suddenly Toby stopped talking in the middle of a sentence and nudged Garrett. They both were looking in the direction of two men who were standing on the edge of the crowd.

Tripper thought one of the men looked liked some kind of bird. He had a thick neck and a skinny, bald head that came to a point with a few tufts of black hair sticking up. A vulture! she told herself. And the other one, who was short with red hair, had an unpleasant smile. He looks like a hyena, Tripper thought.

Tripper's father went over to Toby and

Garrett to find out what was wrong. It was clear that neither one of them would say another word as long as those two men were around. Roger Tripper went to ask the two men to leave.

Usually Leroy would have done a job like that. Leroy was quite good at it, but Leroy was in London.

The two men refused to budge. Roger Tripper became more and more polite. The men started making fun of him. Nick went over and one of the men gave Nick a shove. In no time at all Gene was at the scene — and Sam, too. Tripper was afraid there was going to be a fight.

"Oh honestly," Coco said. She marched over and pushed past the film crew. "Shoo!" she said to the two men with a wave of her hand.

The men stared down at Coco in surprise. They looked at each other. A moment later they were gone.

Everyone had to wait for Garrett to stop laughing before they could continue the interview.

The film crew broke for lunch. Roger Tripper invited everyone — including Garrett and Toby — to a restaurant right in the center of the row of brightly colored buildings across from the big clock tower.

They sat at a light wooden table on benches with high backs right by the window.

Roger Tripper smiled at Toby, who was staring around at the plants hanging from the ceiling and at the waitresses in their green-and-white aprons. "Haven't you been in here before?"

"Never been in a restaurant," Toby mumbled.

Sam ordered mince collop pie. Tripper decided to try it, too.

"What do you like to eat?" Tripper's father asked Toby.

"Other than sweets?" Toby asked hoarsely.

Roger Tripper laughed. "Well, we'll have the sweets later," and he pointed to a counter that was filled with beautiful-looking pastries, cakes, and other desserts.

The mince collop pie was delicious. It was made of meat, onions, parsley, and gravy in a puffed pastry. At Toby's suggestion everyone ordered a drink called Orange Squash. It was quite sweet.

Everyone was talking except Coco. She

had ordered smoked salmon with dill, but she was only eating the dill.

Sam was sitting next to Garrett. "Who were those two men?" Sam asked. "Are they from Mull?"

"No," Garrett said. "They're from an independent salvage ship that lies right off Bloody Bay — outside the harbor. They're divers, too, but they go after wrecks that no one has claimed. Very often they sell the artifacts they find at very high prices to the illegal market. They pick over the bones of old ships. That's why those salvage ships are called the vultures of the sea."

"And," Toby said, "those two come poking around trying to make us kids tell them what we've seen. They were over at MacBrayne's Pier this morning, telling us they didn't believe those pumps were broken. They thought something else was going on — that you found something," he said to Garrett.

It turned out that the men had offered Toby and his friends all sorts of things — lollies, Orange Squash, and other sweets to tell them what they had seen or heard.

". . . and those chocolate marshmallow tea cakes," Toby said sadly, "the ones that taste better if you smash them in the wrapping first."

"Ah yes," Garrett said softly. "We used to do that."

"But we didn't say anything to them," Toby told Garrett. "Divers have to keep their mouths shut," he said proudly.

Garrett grinned at Toby.

After lunch they went back to finish shooting the interview. Toby asked Garrett how divers made money and Garrett explained that, very often, they weren't paid anything at all — except a small allowance — but, if they found any treasure, they would get a share of it.

"On some dives we are searched every time we come to the suface," he said, "to make sure we aren't taking anything for ourselves."

When the interview was over, Tripper saw Garrett go over to Coco and say something to her. She was trying to pack the lights into a metal case. But she was so flustered, she was putting them all in the wrong way. None of them fit. Tripper felt sorry for her.

Gene called Tripper over. "Sam and I

are going to do some fishing this afternoon. We'll try to get a boat off the Mishnish Pier. Want to come?"

"Thanks," Tripper said, "but I already told Coco I'd go shopping with her." Coco liked shopping more than anything in the world.

Sam was logging in the tape of the interview. When he finished, he handed the boxes to Tripper. "Will you take these up to the hotel for me?" he asked.

Tripper nodded and put them in her shoulder bag. When she passed Coco, she saw that Coco was still fumbling with the lights. Garrett was watching her and smiling. He didn't seem aware that he was the one who was making her confused.

"I'll pack the lights," Tripper whispered. Coco nodded and stood up.

Tripper heard Garrett say to Coco, "Well, where are you off to this afternoon?"

There was no answer. Tripper looked up. Coco's face was bright red. She seemed completely tongue-tied. She stared down at her feet and started fiddling with the tools that hung on a big belt around her waist.

"I'm . . . going . . . tripping with Shopper," Coco mumbled, and she turned an even brighter shade of red. "I . . . mean . . . I'm going flopping with Flipper."

Coco suddenly spun around and hurried away up to the hotel.

Garrett stood there looking after her.

Coco's Dream

When Tripper got up to the hotel, she found Coco sitting in a room called the Conservatory.

The Conservatory was a delightful room that seemed suspended above the harbor. It was all glass windows designed like a hothouse. There were white wicker chairs and tables. Coco was sipping a cup of tea and, at the same time, writing in a little red book with a magnetic pencil.

Tripper didn't want to disturb her. She started to leave, but Coco caught sight of her.

"Wait, Tripper," Coco said. "I've got to talk to you."

Tripper sat down across from Coco in a white wicker chair.

"Oh, what am I going to do?" Coco said. "Every time he says anything to me, I get my words all mixed up. I don't know what to say. And there's something else. . . ."

Coco leaned forward. Her dark eyes, which usually sparkled with excitement, looked dull and haunted.

"Tripper," she said, "you've got to read this." She pushed the little red book over to Tripper. "It's my dream diary. Start at the beginning."

Tripper looked at it. "Are you sure you want me to read it?"

Coco nodded. "You have to. You see, I started having these strange dreams when we began this film on diving for treasure. The first dream I had was when we were shooting a salvage operation in the South China Sea. That was in January." She flipped back to the first entry. "There," she pointed. "Read it, Tripper."

Tripper read the first entry. She looked up at Coco in wonder. "But that's just like the Spanish princess."

"I know." Coco looked frightened.

It seemed that Coco had a dream that, when she was working on this film, she would meet the man she would fall in love with. She kept seeing this stranger in her dream.

"Now read the one I had in Malta," Coco said.

Once again Coco had had the same dream. "... and off the coast of Japan ... and in the Virgin Islands." Coco flipped the pages of the little red book.

"I didn't have the dream again for a few weeks — until the night we arrived in Mull," Coco went on. "That night I had the same dream and the next day I met Garrett," Coco said in a hushed voice. "Tripper, *he was the man in the dream*."

Tripper sighed and looked out the window at Garrett, who was leaning against the stone wall talking to Sam.

"Coco," she said, "it's just like a fairy tale. Maybe you can't talk straight because you're under a spell!"

When she looked back at Coco, she saw that Coco's eyes were filled with tears. Coco whispered, "I'm so afraid something will happen to him. I had another dream last night." She turned to the latest entry in the diary and handed it to Tripper.

Garrett told me that he had located the treasure, but it wasn't where it was supposed to be; it wasn't in the area of the search. Somehow, it had been hidden in another part of the harbor. He said that treasure chests containing the pay of the entire Spanish fleet were lying right off Calve Island — by the underwater cliff. . . .

Tripper looked at Coco. "Is there really an underwater cliff?" she asked.

"Yes," Coco said. "It's over there." She pointed across the harbor. "It falls off from eighty feet to 150 feet. The currents are very strong. A lot of divers have been lost there. It's very dangerous."

Tripper had the feeling someone had entered the Conservatory. She turned around and saw DeDe Simone standing in the doorway. She was carrying a manila envelope.

"Coco," DeDe said, coming over to the table. "May I talk to you a moment — in private?"

Coco looked disturbed. "Tripper and I are on our way out," she said. "This isn't a very good time."

But DeDe had already pulled over a

chair and was taking a photograph out of the envelope. She placed it on the table. Then she turned and looked steadily at Tripper. "Do you mind? I'd rather talk to Coco alone."

Tripper looked at Coco. Coco was staring down at the photograph. Her face was deathly pale.

Tripper decided to stay right where she was.

DeDe glared at Tripper. Then she turned her back on Tripper and murmured to Coco, "I don't really understand how I got this shot, but I'm afraid it's some sort of warning."

Tripper jumped to her feet and went over to look at the photograph.

Garrett was alone on the ledge, looking out over the harbor with his back to the camera. Looming over him was a blurry shape that looked like a wisp of smoke or a figure.

Coco suddenly pushed back her chair and, without a word, left the Conservatory. Tripper hurried after her.

She caught up to Coco at the front desk.

"Are you all right?" Tripper asked. She felt quite shaken herself.

"Fine!" Coco's eyes were bright and her cheeks were pink. "It's all so ridiculous!" she said. "Now, come on, Tripper. Time to go shopping. I just have to go upstairs and change my clothes."

Coco led Tripper to the foot of the stairs.

"I never trusted that DeDe Simone," Coco whispered to Tripper. "I'm simply not interested in those ghost photographs she takes. Everyone knows there are no ghosts on Mull."

"Oh no?" Tripper asked with amusement. She would have expected Coco to believe in ghosts.

"No ghosts," Coca said cheerfully. "Just fairies. That reminds me. I have to check on that milk."

"What milk?" Tripper asked.

Coco was already hurrying up the dark wooden staircase. The grandfather clock was striking the half hour.

Tripper was pleased that Coco was behaving more like her old self. "You see," Coco explained as they went up the stairs, "on Mull you always leave out a glass of milk for the fairies. But you have to keep in mind that there are two kinds of fairies

— first there are the household fairies called the *glaistig*. The *glaistig* are the helpful fairies, but they can be mischievous, too. Even if you leave out a glass of milk for them, you never know what they will do. Sometimes they will clean up your house and make it nice and tidy, but other times they will throw everything around and make a terrible mess."

"What are the other fairies like?" Tripper asked. "You said there were two types of fairies."

"The other fairies on Mull are green and they only have one nostril," Coco said. "They mostly foretell doom and disaster."

"So we don't leave any milk out for them — right?" Tripper asked.

"No, we don't," Coco said. "We try not to get mixed up with them at all."

Coco's room was in the turret — across from Tripper's room. Outside her door was a half-drunk glass of milk.

"Oh good!" Coco said. "They've been here." She threw open the door to her room.

Coco's room was quite tidy, even though there were piles of brand-new wool sweaters, Scottish plaids, books, and gifts on the bed and both chairs. Apparently Coco had already done quite a lot of shopping.

"You see," Coco said. "It's all cleaned up."

"But don't you think the maids cleaned up?" Tripper asked.

"Never," Coco said. "I gave the maids strict orders not to touch this room so that we could give the *glaistig* a chance." Coco looked around happily. "Now I just have to change, and — " Suddenly she gasped. "Oh no! I must have left my dream diary downstairs."

Coco started down the stairs. "I'll be right up," she called back to Tripper.

A maid passed her on the stairs. "They've been here!" Coco cried.

"Yes, miss," the maid said. When she passed Tripper in the hallway, she smiled. Tripper was quite sure she detected traces of a milk moustache on the maid's upper lip. But Coco hadn't seemed to have noticed anything. She was on her way down the stairs, singing a Scottish tune:

I had a dream the other night. . . .
Lowlands, lowlands away.

Tripper went across the hall to her room.

She opened the door and hung her shoulder bag on a big hook on the back of the door. On the tea table next to the door there was a playing card leaning up against the electric tea kettle. Tripper wondered how it got there.

She decided to do a little unpacking, but when she looked around, she saw that someone had already unpacked for her.

All her bags were pulled open. Her belongings were strewn all over the room. The drawers to the big chests had been pulled open.

Tripper walked into the bathroom and saw that her camera bag had been opened, too. The contents had been dumped all over the floor — her darkroom supplies, her lenses, her camera filters. . . .

Tripper stared at the mess.

There was a knock on her door.

"Tripper!" Sam called. "Coco's looking all over for some diary. She can't find it. She's tearing the hotel apart. She wants to know if you have it."

Tripper opened the door for Sam. Sam stared around the room at the mess. "What happened?" he asked.

Tripper didn't say anything.

"We'd better call the police," Sam said.

"Don't be silly," Tripper said. "We can't report fairies to the police." She felt a little dazed. "But you know, Sam, it doesn't seem very fair of them. They didn't even give me a chance. I only found out a few minutes ago about leaving that milk. . . ."

"Tripper," Sam said. "What in the world are you talking about?"

". . . of course it might be those other fairies." Tripper was having a hard time sorting out fairies. Suddenly she came to her senses. "Oh, never mind," she said to Sam. "Just something Coco said." She looked around. "It doesn't seem very friendly, does it?"

Sam was looking at the playing card on the tea table. "No," he said slowly, "it doesn't seem friendly at all. Someone left you the nine of diamonds."

"Well, it's just a playing card," Tripper said. "What bothers me is — "

"I don't like it," Sam said. "The nine of diamonds is known as the Curse of Scotland. The orders for the massacre at Glencoe three hundred years ago were supposed to have been written on the nine of diamonds."

Sam picked up the card and turned it over. Suddenly he looked up at Tripper.

"Tripper," he said, "where are those negatives? The negatives of Lachlan Maclean. Did you leave them in this room?"

"Well, no," Tripper said. "They're in my shoulder bag. I had them with me."

Tripper went and got her shoulder bag. She reached inside. "Oh, I forgot," and she handed Sam the tapes of the interview.

Sam put them on the tea table and said impatiently, "The negatives. *Are the negatives there?*"

Tripper reached into the side pocket and pulled out the glassine envelope with the negatives.

"Here they are. Wait a minute...." She stared at Sam. "Do you think someone came in here looking for *these*?"

"Tripper," Sam said quietly. "There is something written on the back of this card. Look."

On the back of the nine of diamonds was a message. It was written in big red letters.

"THE FACE IS MINE," it said.

Second Sight

Tripper and Sam were having a heated argument.

"You've got to tell the police," Sam was saying. "This room was broken into."

"It was all my fault," Tripper said. "I left the door unlocked. The key was right in the door."

"That doesn't matter," Sam said. "It's a crime. Things like that don't happen here. There's almost no crime on Mull. I heard the biggest crime was poaching salmon."

"What's wrong with cooking fish?" Tripper asked.

"Not cooking them, Tripper. Stealing them. Stealing them from private streams." Sam paused. "Now, come on,

Tripper. The police station isn't far from here."

"What am I going to say to them?" Tripper asked crossly. "I suppose you want me to walk in there and say, 'Well, at first I thought it was the fairies, but now I realize it was only the ghost of Lachlan Maclean who came busting into my room, looking for his face!'" Tripper groaned. "They'll laugh their heads off."

DeDe Simone stood outside the door, listening. A part of her was enjoying hearing the two friends argue, but she didn't have much time. She stood in the dim hallway and once again read the entry in Coco's little red diary:

Garrett told me he'd located the treasure, but it wasn't where it was supposed to be. . . .

So that was the reason the dive had been called off. The pumps weren't broken. They were planning to move those pumps across the harbor — to Calve Island near the underwater cliff. It sounded quite dangerous. No wonder the photograph had frightened Coco.

DeDe was surprised Garrett had confided in Coco. Divers were sworn to secrecy; she knew that. But what amazed DeDe Simone the most was that she had taken that photograph of Garrett and the specter on the ledge before she even knew he had located the treasure of the Tobermory Galleon!

The newspapers would be very interested in that photograph. She had quite a story. She was beginning to wonder if she ought to call a press conference. She was pretty sure the photograph would prove that she also had the gift of "second sight," but she would have to check the definition in her *Dictionary of the Supernatural.*

DeDe closed the little red diary. Just then she heard voices on the stairs. Her family had returned from the golf course. She tried to figure out how to get rid of that diary.

"Don't you see, Sam," Tripper was saying. "I can't show the police these negatives. I can't show them to anyone until I figure out what happened. If I report this to the police, and don't show them the negatives, I will be withholding evidence. Oh, come on, Sam, help me clean up the mess in the bathroom. I hope nothing is broken."

"I still think you should tell the police," Sam muttered.

Their voices had gotten fainter. DeDe pushed the door to Tripper's room open a crack and quickly laid the diary on top of some boxes on the small tea table near the door. She pulled the door until it was almost closed and crept down the hallway to the staircase.

Things were beginning to take shape.

Patterns

Sam sat on the rocks of the main quay and watched the comings and goings of the small fishing village. He felt perfectly content.

The town of Tobermory was bustling with activity. There were the people doing their marketing — at the butcher's, the fish market, the pastry shop. There were the tourists visiting all the gift shops. And then there were the families from the sailboats, dressed in their yellow oilskins, walking up and down Main Street, peering into the shops, reading all the menus on the tea shops and the notices on the bulletin board of the community hall.

Sam felt as if he were watching a stage set. He saw Coco and Tripper making their way along the waterfront — going in and out of the brightly colored shops — The Treasure Chest, Togs and Clogs, The Craft Centre. . . . Coco stopped often on the sidewalk. She seemed to know most of the townspeople and she introduced them all to Tripper.

The fishermen were laying out big orange nets on the rocks. Sam liked watching them. Gene had had no luck getting a boat to go out fishing that afternoon. Toby had offered to take Gene fishing on MacBrayne's Pier where he and his small friends spent their time jigging for fish. Sam could see them from where he was sitting. He could also see Garrett and the dive supervisor talking on the pier. As he watched, they climbed into Garrett's small motorboat and headed out toward the barge with the big pumps.

Sam watched them out on the barge. He suddenly had an odd feeling. He turned around and scanned the waterfront. He looked up. High on a hill behind the row of shops, he could see a figure with high-powered binoculars. Then he noticed on the hill to the south of Tobermory another figure with binoculars. Both sets of binoculars seemed to be trained on Garrett and the dive supervisor out on the barge.

Sam recognized the men. They were the divers from the independent salvage ship — the men who had given the film crew such a hard time that morning.

Coco and Tripper had come to the end of the row of shops. They were loaded down with shopping bags. Coco couldn't think of another thing to shop for.

"We've run out," she said to Tripper. "Let's see if anyone wants us to do some shopping for them."

Tripper shrugged. "Fine," she said. She always enjoyed shopping with Coco. Coco always asked the shopkeepers lots of questions before she bought anything. She called it "shopping in depth."

"We'll make a list," Coco said, and she took out her red dream diary with the magnetic pencil. "I'm so glad you found this," she said to Tripper.

"I'm still trying to figure out how it got on my tea table," Tripper said.

"Well, I'm just glad it's found. You see, I also write my shopping lists in it." Coco sighed. "Before I started dreaming about Garrett, most of my dreams were just shopping lists."

They walked across Main Street and out onto the pier to see if Sam wanted anything.

"Just a postcard for Binker," Sam said. "But I'd rather pick it out myself." Sam always sent his dog postcards from location.

Coco and Tripper stopped off at Mac-Brayne's Pier next.

"I know!" Coco said as soon as she saw Gene fishing with Toby and his friends. "A new fishing outfit. You need a new fishing oufit."

Gene didn't look up. "Never," he muttered. Gene always fished in the same clothes — old jeans and a torn blue T-shirt.

"Well, you must need something," Coco said. "What about some nice new fish hooks or those shiny things?"

"Lures?" Gene asked.

"Yes," Coco said. "I think I will buy you a lure for a present. That will be interesting to shop for." She sat down next to Gene and started making notes. "Now all you have to do is to tell me a little about these fish you are interested in. What are their habits? What do they like to do?"

Gene looked up and grinned at Coco. "They like to swim," he said.

"They . . . like . . . to . . . swim," Coco wrote in her book.

Tripper saw Garrett and the dive supervisor coming onto the dock. She waved to Garrett and he waved back. He tied up the boat and went over to Coco.

Tripper sat down next to Toby, who was jigging for fish. "You have to be careful not to make the fish dizzy," he explained to Tripper.

Just then Coco came over and grabbed Tripper. "Quick!" she said. "We have more shopping to do. Garrett just asked if he could take me to the *ceilidh* tonight. It's a big dance in the community hall. We have to buy some books on Scottish country dances right away. They look much harder than square dances. Everyone on the floor does the same thing at the same time. Maybe we should buy some records, too. . . ."

Sam saw that the two men were no longer watching from the hills. A few minutes later, however, he saw them standing under the big clock tower in the center of town. They seemed to be waiting for something. When Garrett walked by, the two men took off separately after him. Sam noticed that they kept a good distance. It was clear they didn't want Garrett to see them.

Garrett did a few errands. He went into the hardware store and into a shop that sold diving equipment. Finally he went into the hotel where he was staying, the Mishnish Arms.

The two men hung around the hotel for a while. Then one of them walked along the waterfront and went into the red public phone booth that was closest to MacBrayne's Pier. Sam saw the other man go into the public phone booth at the other end of the harbor.

Sam watched them for a while. He was puzzled. Then all at once he realized they were talking to each other. They were talking from one public phone booth to the other. They were using the public phones as walkie-talkies. And, all the while, they were waiting for Garrett. . . .

"Vacation's over!" Sam looked up. Gene

was standing in front of him. "Back to work," Gene said with a grin. "Roger wants to hear the tapes of the interview this morning."

Sam got to his feet. He wondered what the two men could hope to learn by following Garrett.

Coco and Tripper had tea at the same restaurant where they had eaten lunch. Coco didn't say much. She was studying the books on Scottish country dancing that she had bought. The books were full of diagrams that looked very complicated.

Tripper had bought a book, too. It was a book about Duart Castle. There was a reproduction of the portrait of Lachlan Maclean that hung in the Banquet Hall.

"Clue number one," Tripper told herself. "It is not a photograph of a man; it is a photograph of a portrait."

She looked at Coco, who was using her fingers to try to work out the steps pictured in one of the books.

"Coco," Tripper said, "I think I'll go up to David MacKinnon's darkroom. I have some negatives I want to print."

Coco sighed and closed the book. "I'll go

with you," she said. "I want to see David MacKinnon. Maybe he can teach me some of these Scottish dances. And he promised to draw me a map of a place on the moors where people have heard the fairies sing."

As they were getting ready to leave, Tripper looked out the window and saw DeDe Simone waiting outside one of the red public phone booths. She was holding a manila envelope. DeDe looked very impatient.

DeDe tapped on the glass for the second time. "If you don't mind," she said to the short man with red hair who had been in that booth for almost forty minutes. He smiled at her, but he didn't look friendly; he looked as if he wanted to kill her.

DeDe looked at her watch. She had made a list of all the important newspapers she had seen in the newsstand. It was Saturday afternoon and she hoped she could reach a reporter at the city desk.

There was another phone booth at the other end of the harbor, but it was tied up, too. She couldn't use the phone at the hotel. Her father was trying to reach his country club back home; he wanted to know the golf scores of a tournament that had been held.

There was a missing pane of glass in the booth. DeDe stepped closer and listened.

". . . can't get the story out of anyone," the man was saying. "I don't think the pumps are broken; I think they're covering up. . . ."

DeDe had a feeling this man was a newspaper reporter. She listened some more. ". . . we'll try to get the story out of Garrett later tonight. I was thinking about a nice little interview — after dark." The man smiled his strange smile.

Now DeDe was sure he was a reporter. She didn't have to waste time calling newspapers. There was a reporter right in the phone booth.

She tapped on the glass again.

"May I talk to you a moment?" DeDe called through the pane of broken glass. "I may have some information that would interest you. Of course the pumps aren't broken. . . ."

As it turned out, the man was very interested. When he saw the photograph of Garrett, he agreed with DeDe that it seemed to suggest danger — a warning. He was also amazed that DeDe had taken it before she even knew Garrett had located the treasure.

"I'll bet they'll want it on the front page of the *Times* tomorrow," he said to DeDe.

"The *Times*?" DeDe asked. "You work for the London *Times*?"

"What else?" The man smiled at her. His smile reminded DeDe of an animal — a weasel? No, a hyena.

"Now," he went on, "tell me more about these treasure chests they've located off Calve Island."

"Well," DeDe began as they walked past the big clock tower, "that part has to be kept out of the paper right now. It has to be kept secret until they announce it."

"Of course," the man murmured.

"But, you see," DeDe went on, "Garrett and I are quite close and he was saying. . . ."

A Jig-Saw Puzzle

Sam was sitting in the Conservatory of the Western Isles Hotel with Gene and Roger Tripper. They were listening to the tapes of the interview that had been filmed that morning with Garrett and Toby.

Roger Tripper was called to the hotel telephone. A minute later he came back. "It's Tripper," he told Sam. "She wants to talk to you. She and Coco are going to have dinner at David MacKinnon's house."

The hotel telephone was in the hall in a small booth. Sam picked up the phone. He could hear Scottish music in the background.

"What's going on?" he asked Tripper.

"David MacKinnon and Toby are teaching us the setting step for the *strathspey*,"

Tripper said. "I haven't even been in the darkroom yet."

"What's the *strathspey*?" Sam asked.

"It's a Scottish dance," Tripper explained. "David wants to know if you can come up for dinner."

"Can't," Sam said. "We've got to listen to some more tapes. I think we're going to have dinner right in town."

"I'll look at the negatives after dinner," Tripper said.

"Hold on, Tripper." Sam was having trouble hearing her. There was a racket going on in the small waiting room outside the booth.

DeDe and Phyllis Simone were having a fight. It sounded like a fairly typical fight in the Simone family.

They were fighting about a can of hair spray.

"I don't see why you don't buy your own hair spray," Phyllis was saying. "I need mine back."

"Well, it's too bad," DeDe said coldly. "I left it up in the darkroom. You know, Phyllis, there are more important things than your hair."

"Like your photography?" Phyllis said.

"I want my hair spray now." Phyllis's voice had gotten quite shrill. "I need it. You know, DeDe, if you don't get it, I'm going to tell on you."

Sam waited. The fight seemed to have stopped.

"Okay, Tripper," he said. "Now I can hear you."

"What was that all about?" Tripper asked.

"DeDe and Phyllis were having a fight," Sam said.

"What about?" Tripper asked.

"A can of hair spray. Sounds typical."

"Hair spray?" Tripper asked. "They were fighting about hair spray?"

"Yes, apparently DeDe took Phyllis' hair spray." Sam paused. "I don't see why she would. DeDe doesn't look as if she uses it."

"No, she doesn't," Tripper said thoughtfully.

"Well, got to go," Sam said. "Your father and Gene are waiting for me. I'll come up there later."

Sam went with Gene and Roger Tripper for dinner at the Captain's Table. On the way to dinner they bumped into Coco, who was returning from David MacKinnon's, skipping.

She did a little jig as she talked to them. "I can't stop now," she said breathlessly, "or I'll forget the steps. This is the setting step for the reel."

When they finished dinner, it was getting dark. The town of Tobermory was filled with the sound of music — accordian, fiddle, pennywhistle — coming from Aros Hall. The *ceilidh* had begun.

On the way back to the hotel, they saw Garrett and Coco on the way to the dance. Garrett was wearing a kilt and a white shirt. He looked very handsome. Coco looked happy and excited.

It was almost ten-thirty before Sam, Gene, and Roger Tripper settled down in the Conservatory again to listen to the rest of the tapes.

Everything was fine until they got to the last reel.

Garrett and Toby were discussing the business of diving for treasure when suddenly Garrett's voice started dropping in and out very rapidly. His voice sounded hollow and wobbly. He sounded as if he were underwater.

"I don't understand it," Gene said. "It's only on this reel."

There was also a thud on the tape. Sam felt his heart beating fast — almost in time to the thud.

"It goes in cycles," Gene said. "It sounds like a spoke on the reel."

Roger Tripper sat up straight. "A spook?" he asked.

"No, no, no," Gene said. "A spoke."

"Oh, of course." Roger Tripper looked very puzzled. "How did we get a spoke on the reel?"

"I don't know," Gene said.

Sam knew perfectly well that a spoke was a technical problem. But he had never actually heard one before. For some unexplained reason, the tape had been demagnetized. Every time he heard the eerie distortion on Garrett's voice, he felt his skin crawl. So many odd things had been happening.

Sam turned to Roger Tripper. "Did Eva ever mention a spot of bright light that appeared on only one frame of the footage Nick took of the Western Isles Hotel?"

"No," Tripper's father said, "but I'm sure she told Nick about it."

"It was right on that ledge," Sam said, "the ledge where we filmed the interview."

Roger Tripper was quiet. He and Sam sat there, looking out at the ledge.

It was one thing for ghosts to show up in DeDe's spirit photographs; it was another thing when they started popping up on motion picture film and sound tracks. Sam was beginning to wonder if that ledge *was* haunted.

Tripper turned on the enlarger light and looked at the blowup of the negative on the darkroom easel. She focused on the grain.

She had another clue. Every exposure was different. Lachlan Maclean's face got lighter and lighter in each negative until it almost faded out of the clouds in the last one.

Tripper decided she would print every negative. She might not learn anything from it, but she enjoyed printing. It helped her think.

David MacKinnon's darkroom was in a small cottage across from the main house, which had once been a vicarage. There were a few other small cottages on the grounds, surrounded by old trees and a big garden.

The darkroom was lit only by a yellow safelight. Tripper held the negatives up to the light and found the first one. As she was slipping the negative into the negative carrier, she felt something on the edge of the negative that she hadn't noticed before.

Right near the sprocket hole was a tiny V-shaped cut — a notch. It was to mark the film — to be able to load it in the dark. "Or reload it," Tripper told herself, "and line up the first shot exactly."

Suddenly she noticed something else. She bent over the easel with the magnifying glass and studied the pattern of dots of the blowup. Lachlan Maclean did not really blend into the clouds. There was a definite outline around his face.

Tripper turned off the enlarger light and stood there thinking. After a minute, she went and turned on the overhead light. She walked over to a large display board and studied the photographs.

DeDe had created a little gallery of her spirit photographs. Tripper looked at the blur on the ledge in the first photograph — the one she had seen on the ferry. Then she moved over and looked at the photograph of Garrett on the ledge. The blur in that photograph had exactly the same shape as the first one — almost like a piece in a jig-saw puzzle. Tripper had a feeling it would match the outline around Lachlan Maclean's face. "A cutout," she told herself.

She knew she was on to something. If only she could fit the pieces together. She turned off the overhead light and went back to the enlarger. She bent over the magnifying glass and tried to follow the outline in the clouds. She was deep in concentration when a voice behind her said:

"But he doesn't belong there."

Tripper jumped. She turned around. DeDe Simone was staring down at the blowup on the easel.

"Of course he doesn't belong there," Tripper snapped. "Nobody belongs there. Faces don't belong in clouds." Tripper did not like being sneaked up on.

Then she realized that DeDe had said something different. She had said, "But he doesn't belong *there*."

"DeDe," Tripper said quietly, "where *does* he belong?"

DeDe didn't answer. She walked over to

one of the cabinets and took something out and wrapped it in her cable-knit sweater. But Tripper had already seen it. It was a can of hair spray.

"You know, DeDe," Tripper said casually. "If I wanted to make a spooky shape — sort of smoky and blurry — on a photograph, do you know what I might do?"

"I'm not really interested," DeDe said, but she waited for Tripper to go on.

"I would cut a tiny shape out of a piece of black paper and cover the lens. Then I would spray it with something — maybe hair spray — and remove the paper." Tripper was very pleased with herself.

DeDe just stared at Tripper in stony silence.

"Now, DeDe," Tripper went on in a pleasant voice, "where does he belong? Where does Lachlan Maclean belong?"

DeDe didn't say anything.

All at once Tripper made a wild guess. "Does he belong on the ledge? Does Lachlan Maclean belong on the ledge?"

"I haven't the faintest idea what you're talking about," DeDe said.

"That's it!" Tripper said. She went back

to the enlarger. "So, what we have here is a double exposure. You'd already been to Duart Castle and taken a roll of the portrait of Lachlan Maclean through a cutout. You wound it back to the beginning and packed it in the box as if it were a fresh roll of film."

Under the yellow safelight, DeDe's eyes seemed to glitter with hatred for Tripper.

"You were planning to reload it, guided by that notch you had made, and shoot a double exposure on the ledge with the stone wall. It would then appear that Lachlan Maclean was haunting the salvage operation on the Galleon."

Tripper was beginning to feel like a detective in a British mystery film. She knew she was sounding like one, too. She began pacing up and down.

"But something went wrong, didn't it, DeDe?" She paused and turned to look at DeDe. DeDe was silently removing the photographs from the bulletin board. Was she admitting defeat?

Tripper started pacing up and down again. "By mistake, I went into your camera bag on the ferry and used that roll of film to shoot the series of Duart Castle. When you found the roll of film missing, you had to change your story. It could no longer be Lachlan Maclean who was haunting that ledge; you had lost your ghost. You also thought I had taken that roll on purpose."

Tripper had her back to DeDe. She was warming up for her final line. "You wrote that note on the nine of diamonds! You wrote, THE FACE IS MINE. The face *was* yours, wasn't it, DeDe?"

Tripper thought it was quite a good line. She waited for DeDe to confess. But when she looked up, DeDe was gone. She had crept out as silently as she had crept in.

And she had taken the negatives with her.

Tripper turned on the overhead light, and looked around. There was one photograph on the display board. It was a photograph Tripper had not seen before.

It was a photograph of the staircase of the Western Isles Hotel. The sunlight was filtering down from the window on the landing above in an eerie way. There was a hand on the banister. On the hand was a ring — an opal and sapphire ring — Tripper's ring. It was the ring that had belonged to Tripper's mother.

There was a hand on the banister, but there was no one at all on the staircase.

"Tripper!" Sam was outside, knocking on the door. "Can I come in?"

Tripper was standing there admiring the way the photograph had been done — admiring the craftsmanship. It was another double exposure. DeDe had obviously taken one shot of the staircase without Tripper. And then she had taken another over that one with the lens partly covered, so that only Tripper's hand on the banister could be seen.

"Are you in there?" It was David Mac-Kinnon's voice.

"Oh yes," Tripper called happily. "Come in," and she continued to admire the photograph.

The light was perfect. The ring seemed to glow with an unearthly light. How lucky DeDe had been to catch the hand at just the right moment.

But Tripper did not really believe in luck in photography. Only very fine photographers had this kind of luck.

DeDe was a genius!

She turned around. David MacKinnon and Sam were standing behind her, looking at the photograph.

"Isn't it brilliant?" Tripper asked. Her eyes were shining. "It's my mother's ghost."

"Tripper," Sam said, "are you all right?"

Suddenly Tripper felt all mixed up. She knew exactly how that photograph had been faked — and yet, at the same time, she wanted so badly to believe. . . .

David MacKinnon was watching her face carefully.

"It's a terrible photograph," he said gruffly. "It's the worst photograph I've ever seen."

Tripper burst into tears.

"There, there, lassie," David said softly. "Hoaxes are cruel. Hoaxes are dangerous."

Night Dive

DeDe was hiding across from the dark-room in a small shop called The Honesty Shop. She had ducked in when she saw David MacKinnon and Sam coming.

She looked around the little shop. There were apples, oranges, fresh eggs, milk, peanuts, and a big glass jar filled with money. No one worked in the shop. There were Honesty Shops all over Scotland.

On the counter there was a list of the different items along with their prices. People were trusted to put the proper amount of money into the glass jar and take out the correct change.

DeDe wished she had picked a different place to hide. The Scots were forever being truthful and honest. They were always trusting other people. It made her quite nervous. DeDe even found it a little bit disgusting.

She looked out the window. To her relief she saw Tripper, Sam, and Mr. MacKinnon leaving the darkroom and heading toward the main house. She slipped the photos and the negatives she had taken from the darkroom behind a small refrigerator.

There was no way she was going to let Tripper expose her — not before her photo appeared in the London *Times*. When photos were published, people believed them.

Coco was having a wonderful time at the *ceilidh*. Garrett was an excellent dancer. In fact all the people in her set seemed to be good dancers. They all did their best to help Coco through the reels and the jigs — giving her little signals and gentle pushes so that she would be in the right place at the right time.

She noticed that they didn't show off much — they didn't add extra flourishes to the steps. Everyone danced gracefully and in time to the music.

Coco decided that Scottish country dancing was the friendliest dancing in the world.

She stood across from Garrett and thought how nice he looked in his kilt. Every dance began with a bow and a curtsy. Courtesy was very important.

Coco heard two chords and knew that it was not another reel; it was a *strathspey*. She and Garrett were the first couple and they cast off and danced down behind their lines.

Coco thought the *strathspey* was a very elegant dance, but it seemed that every time she met up with her partner, she had to turn and dance with someone else.

When she turned to greet her second corner, she found herself facing the short man with red hair — one of the divers from the salvage ship. Tripper was right; he did have a smile like a hyena.

David MacKinnon had told Coco that the most important rule in Scottish dancing was to smile at everyone "as if you mean it. Then your feet will do what they're supposed to do."

Coco began the graceful setting step of the *strathspey* and smiled at the diver as if she were delighted to see him. She didn't miss a single beat.

* * *

Tripper and Sam were sitting in the drawing room of David MacKinnon's house. Roger Tripper was there, too. He listened quietly as his daughter told the whole story of the negatives of Lachlan Maclean. Then he looked at the photograph of the ghostly ring on the banister of the staircase of the Western Isles.

". . . and what infuriates me," David was saying, "is that it's not even original. DeDe copied a very famous ghost photograph. Let me show you."

He reached up and took a book down from a shelf. He handed it to Roger Tripper. "Take a look at both the Raynham Hall photograph and the one of the Tulip Staircase."

Roger Tripper studied the book for a little while. Then he said, "There's even a ring on the banister in this one!" He turned to Tripper. "Do you want to see?" he asked her.

Tripper usually had a very strong sense of curiosity, but she shook her head. "No, thank you," she said, "not right now."

Her father smiled at her.

It was very cozy in the drawing room. There was a big fire in the fireplace. The room was lined with books — books on criminal law in the British Isles; books on photography, and on history.

Sam was sitting in an armchair, staring into the fire. "Mr. MacKinnon," he said slowly, "have you ever come across spirit photography in motion picture film or on sound tracks?"

"Well, no," David MacKinnon said, "but spirit photography was never my specialty. My work with the Border Police was using photographic evidence to solve criminal cases."

There was a knock on the door of the drawing room. Coco and Garrett entered.

"I forgot to take the map you made for me," Coco said, "the map of the place on the moors where the fairies sing. We stopped by on the way back from the *ceilidh* to pick it up."

"We're thinking of taking a picnic up there tomorrow," Garrett said.

David MacKinnon said, "Come in and sit down." Then he suddenly said, "Toby! What are you doing up?"

Toby was right behind Garrett in his pajamas. He was half asleep, but he begged to stay up "just for a wee while — until Garrett leaves."

His grandfather laughed. "Just for a wee while," he said. "Toby spends every Saturday night with me," he explained.

David went through a pile of papers on his desk and found the map he had drawn for Coco. He handed it to Coco with a twinkle in his eye. "Of course, no one has heard those fairies sing for at least fifteen years."

"DeDe has," Toby said suddenly.

"Is that so?" His grandfather seemed very interested.

"Yes, and she told all the kids that she had seen them, too. She said she was going to take pictures of them."

"Well, it won't be the first time in history a young girl has 'documented' the fairies." He turned to look at Tripper. "Have you ever heard of the Cottingley Fairy Photographs?"

Tripper shook her head.

"It was one of the most famous hoaxes of this century." David reached up and took down another book. He handed it to Tripper. "Two young English girls — aged ten and sixteen — claimed they had photographed the fairies at the foot of the garden. Their photographs became an international sensation. Many people swore that they were genuine, including Sir Arthur Conan Doyle, who wrote the Sherlock Holmes stories."

Tripper looked at the photographs of the fairies in the book published by the two girls.

"Double exposure?" she asked.

David shook his head.

"Don't tell me." Tripper's sense of curiosity had returned. "Let me guess."

"Why don't you borrow the book for tonight," David MacKinnon said. "I'm quite impressed with the way you untangled the mystery of those negatives of Lachlan Maclean. You're quite a detective."

Tripper knew it was high praise coming from David, but she sighed. "And, after all my brilliant deductions, I let DeDe get away with the evidence — those negatives with the notch on them."

"Well, hoaxes are very difficult to prove even with evidence," David said.

For a few seconds he just stared into the fire. "But I think I will try to have a talk with DeDe tomorrow — her parents, too. They're in on it in some way; I'm sure of it. It doesn't seem right to let her get away with it. Besides, it could ruin her life."

Coco and Garrett walked along the dark lane, singing. They were singing "Lowlands Away," but neither of them could think of the last verse.

"Let me see," Coco said. "The first verse is 'I had a dream the other night'; the second verse is 'I dreamed I saw my own true love.' ... But I know there's another verse."

Garrett laughed. "Well, we'll just keep walking and singing until we think of it."

They strolled along the waterfront, singing. It was quite late before they gave up and started up to the Western Isles Hotel.

As they were going up the steps along a path that wound up through the trees, they bumped into Sam. He was carrying his tape recorder.

"Where are you going this late?" Garrett asked.

"I have to record some wild sound. Sound effects," Sam told him. "WAVES AGAINST THE ROCKS. I had to wait until everything quieted down."

Garrett nodded and said good-night.

He and Coco continued up the flight of stairs. It was almost pitch dark, but there was a railing. Garrett held onto the railing and Coco held onto Garrett's arm.

"It's funny," Coco whispered. "Every time I have counted these steps, I got a different number. Once I counted 101 steps. The next time I counted 103. . . ."

"Is that so?" Garrett asked. "I'll count them on the way down."

True to his word, Garrett began counting the steps after he had said good-night to Coco. When he reached the thirty-ninth step, he was grabbed from behind. His arms were pinned behind his back and a rough hand clamped over his mouth. He saw the flash of a diving knife in front of his eyes.

"Not a sound, Garrett," a voice whispered in his ear. He recognized the voice of one of the divers from the salvage ship. "We're going to do a little night diving right off Calve Island. . . ."

Garrett tried to pull away, but the knife flashed before his eyes again.

"Don't move or we'll cut off your air —

permanently," said the diver with a cruel smile.

"We know you've located the treasure, Garrett," said the other diver, "and we know you'll be happy to show us where it is. And, by the way, if you don't come up with it, you don't come up at all!"

Sam sat on the rocks at the end of the quay and adjusted his headphones.

"Hello, test. . . . Hello, test. . . . WAVES AGAINST THE ROCKS," Sam said quietly into the microphone.

The first take was spoiled by the sound of a motorboat. Sam turned to see who was going out so late. He saw Garrett's boat leaving MacBrayne's Pier. It surprised him that Garrett was going out without running lights. He wondered what the head diver was checking on so late at night.

Sam waited until the sound of the motor had faded away.

"Hello, test. . . . Hello, test. . . ." Sam began again. "WAVES AGAINST THE ROCKS. . . ."

The next take was fine. Sam sat silently, recording the gentle lapping of the waves against the rocks in Tobermory Bay. . . .

The Moors

Garrett's boat was found early the next morning, adrift by the underwater cliff off Calve Island. There was no one aboard. His diving equipment was gone.

No one could figure out what he had been doing, but within a short time Royal Navy divers were called in. It would be a dangerous recovery operation. And there wasn't much hope that his body would be found.

DeDe left the hotel very early. Her family was still asleep, but she had told them the night before that she was planning to document the fairies on the moors that morning. They had only a few more days on the Isle of Mull and DeDe had worked hard preparing for these photographs.

There was some kind of commotion on

MacBrayne's Pier, but DeDe did not stop to find out what was going on.

It was a quiet Sunday morning. She started up the hill to Craispuir Lane. She was glad she had worn high socks with her flat-heeled pumps. Wellingtons or gum boots were probably better for the moors, but DeDe found them so unattractive with her outfit — her beige A-line wraparound skirt and pink blouse.

She followed the lane until she came to the little narrow valley with rock face on the northeast side. She climbed the low stone wall and headed across the moors to the stone outcropping on the hill. It was the place where, as legend had it, the fairies had been heard to sing.

It was very still. DeDe found herself admiring the blue hairbells, the purple foxgloves, and the yellow gorse.

She would have to include some of these wildflowers in her photographs of the fairies.

Everyone had heard the tragic news about Garrett. The members of Roger Tripper's film crew sat with Coco in the Conservatory, waiting. . . .

Coco sat very still, looking out the window at the recovery operation going on off Calve Island. At one point, she turned to Tripper and said in a dull voice, "I just remembered the last verse of 'Lowlands Away.' 'I dreamed my love was drowned and dead.' " Then she turned back and continued to watch as they searched for Garrett's body.

Tripper felt her throat tighten. Just then David MacKinnon and Toby walked into the Conservatory. Toby's eyes were red, but he just sat down next to Coco and held her hand.

They could hear Missy Simone's voice in the hallway of the Western Isles. "What a terrible thing to happen on our last couple of days on Mull."

David MacKinnon excused himself, and went into the hall to talk to Missy Simone. When he came back, he said to Sam in a low voice, "I'd like to talk to DeDe now. It may not seem like the best time, but there's nothing much we can do about Garrett and I'd like to get it over with. Her mother tells me she went up to the moors to photograph the fairies. She doesn't think DeDe heard the news about Garrett yet."

Sam got to his feet. "Tripper and I will go .get her," he said. "At least we'll be doing something useful."

David MacKinnon drew another map.

DeDe was all set to take her first shot. She had her camera on a tripod and had decided to take a long exposure. She wanted to let in as much light as possible. She needed good depth of field if she was to get both objects in focus — the yellow gorse in the foreground and the cutout of the fairy in the background.

It was at this point that DeDe heard very faint singing. She stopped for a moment and listened. The voices sounded very sweet. It was exactly the way she expected fairies to sound.

There was only one trouble. DeDe Simone did not believe in fairies.

She dropped everything and began to run.

Tripper and Sam reached that spot ten minutes later. They looked around at the paper cutouts and at the photographic equipment spread around on the ground.

"It looks like something scared her," Sam said.

But Tripper was busy admiring one of the paper cutouts that was pinned to a bush. "DeDe's fairies are a lot better than Frances's and Elsie's fairies," she said.

"What?" Sam asked.

Tripper showed him the little crouched grayish-green figure. "I said, 'DeDe's fairies are better than the fairies those two English girls photographed.' More authentic."

"Tripper," Sam said. "We don't have time to discuss artwork. Something scared DeDe. She was running away from something. Look at that."

On the ground were footprints. "Little party-shoe footprints," Sam said. "Tripper, you don't think DeDe came out onto the moors in those little party shoes she and Phyllis always wear."

"I'm sure she did," Tripper said.

Sam followed the footprints back to the low stone wall. "Tripper!" he called. "Come on. We've got to find her."

Tripper took a last look at one of the paper fairies that had been stepped on and crushed when DeDe started to run. Then she went to catch up with Sam.

"It looks as if she started back down the hill to Tobermory and then changed her mind," Sam said as they followed the footprints back to the lane.

Then the footprints suddenly turned up the lane and toward the wildest part of the moors — toward Bloody Bay.

At the end of the lane there was a high stone wall. And, at the top of the wall, hanging from a piece of barbed wire, was DeDe's white cable-knit sweater.

"Hold my tape recorder," Sam said, "and then hand it up to me."

"We're climbing that wall?" Tripper asked, but she took the tape recorder. It was quite heavy.

"Tell me something, Sam," she said. "Why did you bring a tape recorder?"

"I don't know," Sam said. "I guess just in case the fairies *did* sing."

"You were going to record fairies on quarter-inch tape?" Tripper asked.

Sam mumbled something. He was trying to get a good foothold in the stones.

Tripper and Sam were both properly dressed for the moors. They were wearing gum boots, heavy cotton pants, and plaid

ool shirts. But when Tripper followed
Sam over the wall, she wished she had
worn gloves, too.

The ground on the other side fell off
sharply down a steep bank. They picked
up DeDe's footprints again on a sheep path
that led through the heather and gorse.

At last they could see a line of dark pine
trees that David had marked on the map
as Ardsmore Point, and the dark gray
waters of Bloody Bay.

Tripper looked down at the bay. The
ground seemed to slope gently down.
"Maybe DeDe went back to Tobermory
along the coast."

"I don't think it's possible to get around
that way. It's all cliffs and caves. I don't
think there's any beach."

"Well, I think we should take a look,
anyway," Tripper said, and she started
down the hill.

"Wait!"

But Tripper had already put her foot
into gnarled branch. She looked down. She
had stepped into the top of a tree. Right
below her foot was a sheer drop.

It wasn't a hill at all; it was a cliff — a
cliff with trees growing straight out of it.

Tripper had one foot over the edge of a cliff.

Very carefully she untangled her foot from the branch and took a few steps backward.

"We're not used to this kind of countryside," Sam said grimly. "We're going back."

"But we have to take at least one look for her," Tripper said.

"I guess if we could get to a high place. . . ." Sam studied the landscape. "Maybe we could go up through that bracken."

Tripper looked up at a series of hills covered with ferns. The climb looked quite steep. "Let's try," she said.

Sam started off through the bracken and Tripper followed. A third of the way up, she got quite frightened. It was very steep and she didn't trust the ground under her feet. She couldn't see Sam's head at all and she knew she would soon be buried in the bracken. What if she and Sam got separated?

At last she saw Sam's head appear, but not in the place she had expected. She struggled the rest of the way up. She was very overheated and out of breath.

"Time for a rest!" she called, panting hard.

"Nope," Sam said. "The mist is coming in."

"Yes," Tripper said. "It feels nice. It's cooling me off." She looked around. There was no sign of DeDe.

"I don't see Ardsmore Point anymore," Sam said. "But I guess that's the way back." He took off at a fast pace.

There were no sheep paths anymore and the walking was difficult. A few minutes later Tripper said, "I don't remember coming through this marsh, do you?" And then, after a short while, she said, "I don't remember this gully." She felt as if she were going to collapse. "Can't we take a rest?" she called.

"There's a stone wall over there," Sam called back, "but I don't know if it's the same one and I can't tell how far away it is. It's hard to tell distances around here."

The mist was coming in very fast now. All of a sudden Tripper understood the danger. In a few minutes they would not be able to see a few feet in front of them. And they were lost!

Tripper saw the ghost first. She had turned around to see if she could see Bloody Bay. She found herself staring at a grassy knoll about 150 feet away.

At first she thought it was a trick of the light — the sun on a curtain of mist. But then she could make out a shadowy figure following them.

He was dressed in a wet suit and seemed to be running in slow motion. Tripper turned back. She knew it was Garrett. At the same time she knew it couldn't be Garrett. She decided not to say anything.

Tripper began running to catch up to Sam. She slipped and fell into a bog. She had mud up to her waist when she crawled out, but she just stopped long enough to retrieve one of her boots and put it back on.

When she caught up to Sam, he said, "That's better." He seemed very worried. "I haven't the faintest idea where we are. Maybe we should just stop and stay in one place until it clears."

"No!" Tripper said. "I think we should go a little faster."

"Where?" Sam asked.

"Anyplace!" Tripper was almost screaming.

Sam suddenly stopped and listened. Tripper watched his face. She had heard the voice, too. It was calling to them across the moors. It was Garrett's voice, but the voice sounded dead. It had no echo.

Sam scanned the landscape. "Sound hasn't much echo in the mist," he muttered. Then he blinked. He shook his head hard. He opened his eyes and stared.

Tripper slowly turned and followed his gaze. For a brief moment, she saw that shadowy figure of the diver again. Then a thicker mist drifted in and hid the figure.

"Sam," Tripper said calmly. "Does it bother you that, not only are we lost on the moors with the mist coming in, but *we are being chased by a ghost?*"

"Don't be silly, Tripper." But just then Sam caught his breath.

The mist had cleared in the spot where the diver had been, but now Garrett was standing there, dressed in his kilt — the kilt he had been wearing the night before!

Sam turned abruptly and began walking. "Let's go," he said. "We have to get back. We'll try that stone wall over there and see where it leads."

"Yes," Tripper said. "And we have to run very fast."

When they finally reached the stone wall, Sam climbed up to the top and then climbed down again. "It's the wrong one," he said.

Tripper could see the figure in the kilt getting closer. They were trapped. "We're climbing it anyway," she told Sam.

"Wait." Sam was staring out across the mist. But he wasn't looking in the direction of the figure.

"Look at the sheep!" he said suddenly.

"I don't have time to look at sheep right now." Tripper was fed up. "I have to climb this wall."

"But they're moving!" Sam said. "The sheep are moving away from him. They smell him. Don't you see, Tripper? We're downwind of the sheep. They can't smell us. But he's upwind of the sheep and they've caught his scent."

Tripper was furious. "Well, now," she said, "that's a very interesting philosophical question, Sam. I'm so glad you brought it up. 'Can you smell a ghost?' Well, why don't I sit right down here in a gorse bush and write a letter to Katy Bear and ask her to look up the answer to that interesting philosophical question: Can you smell a ghost?"

Sam suddenly grinned. "It's Garrett!" he said.

"I escaped from the salvage ship and swam across Bloody Bay," Garrett told them. "For some reason those two divers thought I had located the treasure of the Galleon by that underwater cliff."

"But that was just Coco's dream," Tripper said.

"They tried to force me to dive out there, but even they could see the waters had gotten too rough," Garrett went on. "Another boat from the salvage ship picked us up. They were going to hold me aboard for another twenty-four hours and try the dive again. No matter what I said, they still believed there were treasure chests of gold down there."

Tripper and Sam were having trouble keeping up with Garrett as they hurried across the moors.

"Are you sure you're all right?" Tripper asked Garrett a few times.

"Of course he's all right," Sam said. "He

was kidnapped and tied up overnight. Then he swam across Bloody Bay, climbed the bluff, and chased us across the moors. He's fine. He's a Scotsman!"

Garrett was more familiar with the countryside. He was carrying the wet suit that he had been wearing over his kilt.

"We've got to get help for that American girl," he said. "A search on the moors can be a very big operation." Garrett led them back to the stone wall at the top of Craispuir Lane.

Sam was the last one over the wall. He had just handed Tripper his tape recorder when he happened to look back.

"I see her," he said. "I see DeDe. Go ahead," he called down. "She's not too far. I'll go get her."

DeDe was sitting among the ruins of an old stone cottage. She was covered with mud. There were scratches and cuts all over her face. Her face was streaked with tears.

Worst of all, her eyes were wild and she was panting. "I heard them sing!" she screamed to Sam. "I heard those fairies sing!"

"That's nice," Sam said. "Let's go." But DeDe refused to stand up. Sam was not feeling very sympathetic toward DeDe. "You heard them sing before and now you heard them again."

DeDe shrieked, "But this time they really *were* singing." And she began to scream.

Sam tried to be patient. "It was probably just your imagination."

"But I don't *have* an imagination!" DeDe yelled. Then she suddenly stopped screaming and began to sob.

Sam agreed with her. In some way DeDe really did not have an imagination. He looked at her.

"DeDe," he said softly. "What were those fairies singing?"

"Hymns," DeDe sobbed. "They were singing 'For the Beauty of the Earth' and songs like that."

"Celtic fairies were singing in English?" Sam asked. "But they have a different language. They come from an older religion. I don't think they would be singing hymns."

DeDe quieted down a little. "I did pass a little church on the way up to the moors."

"Yes," Sam said, "and it's Sunday morning. Sound can carry pretty far around here."

"As a matter of fact, it did get louder when I started down the hill." DeDe was quiet now. After a while, she agreed to get up and go back with Sam.

The police constable wanted to question DeDe immediately. Missy Simone insisted that DeDe change her clothes first, but the police constable said no. DeDe had been seen talking to one of the divers who had kidnapped Garrett.

"But he said he was a newspaper reporter!" DeDe was horrified.

Within an hour their salvage ship — the vulture of the sea — was surrounded and boarded in Bloody Bay. The divers were arrested and charged with kidnapping.

David MacKinnon had a talk with DeDe that afternoon. She told him where she had hidden the photographs and negatives she had taken from his darkroom. But, even though DeDe admitted she had spread a dangerous rumor, she refused to admit she had faked any of her photographs.

"She did, however, tell me that she would

never take another photograph for the rest of her life," David MacKinnon told Tripper.

Tripper was shocked. She found herself thinking that DeDe had chosen too harsh a punishment for herself. . . .

Outtakes

The film crew was having another big Scottish breakfast a few days later at the Western Isles Hotel.

The pumps had been fixed. Once again the search for the treasure of the Tobermory Galleon had begun.

"We're getting great footage," Roger Tripper said, "but we lost a lot of time. The interlock is at the end of August. I spoke to Eva last night and asked her to finish the editing of this sequence in Edinburgh as we film the rest of the salvage operation."

Tripper was surprised that Eva had agreed to come to Scotland. She did not like to leave New York and go on location.

Roger Tripper laughed. "Eva was delighted. You see, her boyfriend Fritz Katzenbach is coming to Scotland. He is going to be playing with the Scottish National Soccer Team in an exhibition game."

He turned to Sam. "I asked her to bring over that trim of the spot of bright light that only appears on one frame. We've got to track down that ghost."

Nick, the cameraman, nodded. "We sure do. I'm no spirit photographer," he grumbled.

"She should bring the outtakes, too," Sam said. The outtakes were the other takes of the same shot — the ones that Eva had decided not to use. "There might be a clue in the outtakes."

Nick said, "I'm almost sure I took that long shot and tilt-up at least four times. And let me see — it was a Sunday evening — Midsummer's Eve, I'm pretty sure of it. It was June 23rd."

Roger Tripper said, "I'm driving to Edinburgh the day after tomorrow to meet Eva and Fritz at the airport and help her get set up. Would you like to come?" he asked Tripper and Sam. "David Mac-Kinnon is coming, too. He's very anxious to have a look at that frame with the spot of light. He's curious about it, but he's got another motive for wanting to come along."

"What's that?" Sam asked.

"David MacKinnon is a great soccer fan. He's hoping to have the chance to meet Fritz Katzenbach!"

Coco was sitting at the table, peacefully writing in her dream diary. At one point she whispered to Tripper, "You know, I think you were right about my being under a spell. As soon as Garrett invited me to the *ceilidh*, I stopped mixing up my words. I could talk straight."

Tripper nodded. "It sounds just like a fairy tale," she said. Tripper was curious. "But are you and Garrett going to . . . um . . . live happily ever after?"

"Oh yes!" Coco's eyes were shining. "We're both thrilled. In September Garrett starts a job diving for a wreck off the coast of Queensland, Australia — the Great Barrier Reef. And I get to go to Greenland. Did you know your father is going to make a film about tracking polar bears?"

"Oh." Tripper was disappointed. That wasn't quite what she had meant by "happily ever after."

Coco sighed. "And then I've been invited to his parents' home in Dumfries, in the Lowlands, for a quiet Scottish Christmas."

Tripper smiled. That was better!

Coco went back to her dream diary. Sam was staring at her. "Do you always use that magnetic pencil when you write in that diary?"

"Of course," Coco said.

"Was the magnetic pencil on the diary when DeDe put it on top of your tea table?" he asked Tripper. "On top of the boxes with the tapes of the interview with Garrett?"

Tripper nodded.

"Gene!" Sam said suddenly.

Gene was concentrating on his Scottish breakfast. He looked up.

"I know it takes a fairly powerful magnet to put a spoke in a tape," Sam said slowly, "but do you think that pencil might have done it?"

Gene looked at it. "It sure could have," he said with a grin. "Looks like we've knocked out another ghost," he said, and he went back to his breakfast.

"This haggis is delicious," he said. "What is haggis, anyway?"

No one at the table said a word.

The airport outside Edinburgh was jammed. There were mobs of soccer fans waiting to welcome Fritz Katzenbach.

Eva got off the plane with him. The first thing she said was, "I brought the negatives of that trim, too. I got them out of the lab."

"Good," Roger Tripper said.

David MacKinnon was introduced to Fritz. Almost at once they were talking about soccer. "I understand you're going to be helping our side beat the Red Devils," David was saying to Fritz as they walked out of the terminal.

Suddenly they were all surrounded by fans. Tripper heard Sam say, "But I don't even play soccer!"

A temporary cutting room was set up in New Town, which was actually quite an old part of Edinburgh. Tripper and Sam watched as David looked at the trim and then screened it on a projector. Then they studied the outtakes — there were no clues. The only thing that was clear was that Eva had chosen the best take of the Western Isles — the steadiest shot where the camera movement was the smoothest.

"Well, I guess there have to be mysteries," Tripper's father said. He was quite disappointed.

That evening they had dinner at the Witchery-by-the-Castle, ". . . the most haunted restaurant in Edinburgh," David MacKinnon told them. They walked down the stairs and into the restaurant.

By the flickering candlelight, they could see, right by the door, a model of a witch in a chair. On the walls were signs of the zodiac, bats, spiders, owls, and horseshoes. There were even witches' spells written there.

They had an excellent dinner. Sam ordered Magic Mushrooms first. ("They're just stuffed," he whispered to Tripper.) Then he ordered duck. Tripper had venison with chestnut, paté, and cherry sauce. There were three kinds of potatoes served with it.

When they finished eating, Roger Tripper said, "I could only get two tickets to the Military Tattoo at the castle tonight. I thought Tripper and Sam should go. The seats aren't even together."

"By all means," David said. "I went to quite a number of Tattoos when I was a boy."

After dinner Tripper and Sam walked up to the castle on the great mass of volcanic rock overlooking the City of Edinburgh. Sam's seat was three rows behind Tripper's in the stadium.

The Military Tattoo was a great display of bands — bagpipes, drums, and fifes. During the Highland sword dance, Tripper suddenly noticed that the Simone family was sitting only a few rows in front of her.

DeDe kept turning around to look at Tripper.

To her surprise, toward the end of the evening DeDe squeezed past the people in her row and sat down next to Tripper.

"Did you know I gave up photography?" DeDe asked.

Tripper nodded.

"And I wanted you to have my camera equipment, but I'm afraid my father got a very good price for it in Edinburgh."

"The Contax, too?" Tripper asked.

DeDe nodded. They were both quiet.

The Tattoo ended with fireworks over

the battlement, high over the stadium. DeDe and Tripper watched them together.

Tripper felt a little funny sitting next to her arch enemy. She felt a little shy. She turned to DeDe when the magnificent display of fireworks had ended and said, "I'm still seeing those fireworks."

"Naturally," DeDe said sharply. "That's because bright light registers on the eye much longer than it actually lasts — you know, like an electronic strobe or a flash cube. A strobe only lasts for the tiniest fraction of a second. The eye sees it for much longer than the camera records it."

"That's true," Tripper said thoughtfully, "and for much longer than one frame of motion picture film. That's it!" Tripper was very excited. She turned to DeDe. "Do you happen to remember when you took that first photograph on the ledge? Was it by any chance Midsummer's Eve, June 23rd?"

DeDe pulled a small notebook out of the pocket of her A-line skirt.

"I guess I should have gotten rid of this, too," DeDe murmured.

"No!" Tripper said. "A photo log is very important."

In the end DeDe got the answer. "Yes, I shot that picture June 23rd, Sunday evening, at nine o'clock."

Nick had been filming the Western Isles at the exact time DeDe had taken her photo on the ledge. And she had used an electronic strobe! That was the spot of bright light on the frame.

"Thank you," Tripper whispered.

DeDe looked surprised.

All the lights in the stadium suddenly went out. DeDe and Tripper stood and listened to the lone piper, playing the bagpipes on the battlements of the castle. Then everyone linked arms and sang "Auld Lang Syne." Tripper felt DeDe slip her arm through hers.

Then they stood for the national anthem, "Scotland, the Brave."

Hark when the night is falling
Hear, hear the pipes a-calling. . . .

When it was over, DeDe went to join her family. Before she left, she slipped a piece of paper into Tripper's hand. Tripper looked at it. It was DeDe's address in the States.

* * *

Tripper and Sam walked back to the hotel through the historic Royal Mile. They stood on the ramp of the Victoria Terrace and looked down at the narrow curved street called West Bow. It was a cobblestone street of old houses, alleyways, and lampposts. A mist was falling.

"You know," Sam said, "this is probably the most haunted street in the world. That's Major Weir's house over there. It's been deserted for years. Someone once spent the sight there and saw a calf's head suspended above his bed."

Tripper was not thinking about ghosts.

"Sam," she said suddenly. "Are DeDe and I alike in any way?"

"Well, you sure act like friends," Sam said.

"How dare you say that!" Tripper was outraged.

"I saw you talking at the Tattoo."

"That was purely professional," Tripper said, and she told him about the strobe. "I'm sure that's the answer to the spot of light on the frame."

Sam was disappointed that there were no more ghosts.

"No, DeDe and I certainly re not friends. We hate each other. I aed you if we were alike?"

Sam didn't answer. He was taring down at the cobblestone street.

"Are we alike?" Tripper demnded. Then she said, "Are you smiling, San?"

"Tripper, did you see that thing flit around that house just now?" Sam sked.

Tripper ignored him.

They started walking back along Victoria Terrace.

"You know," Tripper was saying, "I think I'm going to write to DeDe and tell her that I think it's a crime for her to give up photography. . . ."

"Do you hear faint footsteps behind us on the cobblestones?" Sam asked.

"Yes," Tripper went on, "and, while I'm at it, I'm going to ask her how she lit that portrait of Lachlan Maclean. . . ."

"You know, Tripper, I think those footsteps are getting louder. . . ."